FAMILIARS AND FOES

HELEN VIVIENNE FLETCHER

CHAPTER ONE

*A*deline teetered halfway up the ladder to the attic, the boxes she was carrying pinned between her hands and chin to keep them steady. The rungs themselves were sturdy, their rubber-gripped feet planted firmly on the old wooden floor. It was Adeline's balance that was unreliable, no matter how stable the ground beneath her feet.

Coco let out a whine. He stood at the base of the ladder, his comically big Labrador feet scraping varnish from the floorboards, as he danced in his anxiety to reach her.

"It's okay, puppy," she called to him. She shifted the boxes to a more comfortable position, then slowly climbed the last few rungs up into the storage area in the roof.

Coco gave a resigned sigh and lay down. She could almost hear his thoughts: *Silly hooman, climbing up there. How am I supposed to protect you now?*

Adeline stood, stooping to avoid the sloping roof, and

1

tentatively placed her weight on her right foot. She'd busted her knee during a seizure last week, and Coco had been doing double duty since – keeping her steady when her leg gave way, along with his usual seizure-alert work. A more sensible person would have waited a week, to let it heal, before climbing up into the ceiling, but Adeline had never been one for sticking to the practical. Honestly, she wasn't sure why she'd felt compelled to go on a tidying spree, though her co-workers' jokes about her messy house at lunch today might have had something to do with it.

She sorted the boxes, stacking them against the wall, then rubbed her face, relieved at finally having a hand free to do so. She'd cut her hair to a shoulder-length bob a few weeks ago, thinking it would look cute. Instead, she'd been plagued by the curly, brown strands creeping their way across her face, and sticking to her lip-gloss, every time her hands were occupied.

Determined, she tamed her mop into a ponytail, though one glance at her shadow told her strands were already beginning to escape. Her eyes travelled over the store of boxes scattered around the room, identical to the ones she'd just brought up. This was usually as far as her organising efforts got. She could pack her parents' stuff up, but she could never quite bring herself to get rid of it. The shed outside was full too.

Coco gave another little harrumphing sigh, and the floor underneath him creaked as he curled up. The sound bounced around the room, before falling into silence.

Adeline was always struck by the eerie stillness of the air up here. She supposed the same could be said of any space shut off from people ninety percent of the time, but as a child, she'd been convinced there was something magical up here. Good magical or scary magical, she wasn't sure, but either way, the weight of it hung in the room. Though these days, it was surpassed by the weight of chores unfinished.

The light seemed to fall in strange ways up here, perhaps because of the sloping sides of the roof reflecting the minimal illumination creeping up through the trapdoor. Some areas always fell in darkness, while others seemed to glow, drawing her attention. She caught sight of a box of old clothes, lit by one such pool of light, and couldn't help going over to have a look. Her wardrobe was peppered with an odd mix of pieces from different decades, and attic-rummaging was even more fun than op-shopping.

This was the other danger of coming up here – for every box she put up, there was a good chance she'd bring another back down.

Adeline lifted what she thought was a padded coat from the pile but struggled with the size of it. She took her phone from her pocket, flicking on the torch, and realised her mistake. It wasn't a pile of clothes, but a soft quilt.

It was old, patchworked out of a beautiful mix of faded pink, brown and green floral-patterned fabrics. The seams were visible but neat; hundreds of tiny hand-stitched trails making their way back and forth across the fabric, as if to mark the minutes, hours and days that had been spent working on it.

"Wow," she said aloud. How had she not known this was up here?

She heard Coco move again at the sound of her voice, and glanced towards the trapdoor, but he was already settling down.

She pulled the quilt from the box, stepping back and raising her arms to see the length of it. A more sensible person would have realised before attempting to walk backwards on an uneven surface, in the dark, with a busted knee, that it was not the best idea. Instead, Adeline just realised she was not the most sensible person.

Her heel caught on one of the exposed beams, and her knee buckled, snapping forward. Suddenly, she was careening towards the open trapdoor. She let out a shriek, and threw herself sideways, the quilt tangling between her legs. A tearing sound made her cringe. She hit the floor with a thud, and a cloud of dust rose up around her.

"No, no, no," she whispered.

Coco howled, pawing at the ladder in his attempts to reach her.

"It's okay, Coco!" she called. "I'm okay."

She fumbled for her phone, causing another rip to sound. "Please don't tell me I've..." Adeline trailed off as she saw the line of split threads in the quilt, where two of the carefully handstitched seams had burst open under her grip. She groaned, wondering if perhaps this was the reason it had stayed up here – out of her reach – for so long.

The dust she'd raised seemed to hang in the air, almost in the shape of a person looming over her, as if to say: "See? This is what happens when you try to be tidy!"

Adeline waited, half-expecting the cloud to solidify into a ghost, but the swirls remained faceless. She eased herself up, coughing from the bitter taste in her mouth as the dust settled over her, attaching to her clothes.

Coco let out another howl, and Adeline stood, placing the quilt back in its box where it would be safe from her. "It's okay, puppy. I'm coming."

She made her way back down the ladder, slower this time, as her knee complained about the movement. The dust swirled and coiled around itself again, seeming to follow her path down into the house. Adeline imagined it was ushering her out, happy now her disruptive presence was leaving.

Coco danced around her, as soon as she was on the ground, nudging against her hands and legs.

"Yes, yes, I know. Your mummy is silly, isn't she?" She crouched down, letting Coco lick her face. "Yes, I'm okay, puppy. I'm okay." She stroked his head, the action calming her as much as it did him.

She hooked the ladder and trapdoor back into place, feeling only slightly guilty at leaving the damaged quilt up there. She avoided looking at the photos on the wall in the corridor. She'd lost track of who the ancestors were, but severe moustache-man's eyes seemed to follow her from his frame, disapproving.

She would mend the quilt eventually, she told herself. After she'd finished the pile of too-long hems she'd been meaning to fix, of course. The penalty for being short was a never-ending supply of sewing to do.

She glanced at the time and groaned, all thoughts of mending slipping from her mind. "Come on, pup. We'd better get to the supermarket, or we'll be eating dinner at midnight."

Coco started dancing again, hearing only the word "dinner".

Kate Sheppard was walking down Molesworth Street towards Adeline. Or perhaps floating towards her would be more accurate. The matriarch of New Zealand democracy's feet didn't quite touch the ground, as her transparent figure made its way past her namesake apartments.

The ghost looked up, meeting Adeline's eye. Her Gibson Girl hairstyle and high-necked blouse matched the image Adeline knew from the ten-dollar note, but there was something different in the spirit's expression... a nervousness. Adeline held her breath, frozen for a moment, then she blinked, and the ghost disappeared. Adeline stared into the space where she had been.

It wasn't the first time Adeline had seen the suffragette,

of course, nor was Kate the only apparition Adeline had seen that day. Katherine Mansfield had made her way down Tinakori Road, past Adeline's house, that morning. She presumed the author was on her way to the museum which preserved her childhood home, but she never made it. She always disappeared into nothing a few metres before the "Historic Places" sign.

Adeline had always seen ghosts, or whatever it was they were. She was ten before she realised other people didn't. This was the first time a spirit had made eye contact though, which made Adeline a little uneasy. *Sleep deprivation*, she told herself. She always saw more ghosts when she was tired. She made a mental note to turn off the TV early tonight, no matter how much "just one more episode" called her name.

Coco nudged Adeline's hand with his nose, and she shook her head, doing her best to clear away the thoughts of spirits. She glanced down at Coco and he stared back at her, his eyes solemn while he was in work mode.

"You ready to go to the supermarket?" she asked him. He gave a small tail wag in response.

She made her way slowly up the road to the shop, Coco looking up at her every so often to check she was okay. She smiled back at him, loving seeing his sweet, attentive face peering up at her.

"Good boy," she said, and his tail wagged again.

She grabbed the few things she needed for dinner, not in the mood for a big shop, and ignored the stares of the other customers. Coco, and his assistance dog vest, always drew attention, but his training taught him to ignore it all. Adeline mostly ignored it too, but there were some days, like today, where she just didn't have the energy for dealing with other people. She hoped the stares didn't turn into invasive questions.

She dodged around a family, pretending she didn't notice the little girl's hand reaching out to trail along Coco's fur as they walked past. The mum pulled the girl back and smiled apologetically at Adeline. Adeline gave the most genuine smile she could muster in return. She wasn't sure what was wrong with her lately. She used to have endless patience for explaining assistance dogs to strangers, especially when it came to children. Now, she found interacting with them just made a lonely ache start up in her chest, and she'd have to excuse herself before it spilled over into tears.

She glanced down and felt herself soften seeing Coco's sweet face. She couldn't blame people for approaching, really. Golden Labradors were always adorable, but there was something extra appealing about seeing them take care of people.

Adeline saw a flicker of something misty moving at the end of the aisle, and turned away, no keener to deal with ghosts than with people. But Coco knew her routine: vegetable section, milk, baking aisle, pet food – his favourite – and then bread. He stared at her, and gently pulled towards the bakery, clearly thinking she was confused.

Adeline sighed. He was right, she was being silly. She

needed bread, and the ghosts had never caused her harm. In fact, they usually didn't pay her any attention whatsoever, simply floating nearby, going about their business. She wondered if they were following the routines they'd had in life too – still doing the weekly shop, despite no longer being able to eat the food. If so, she thought she better start doing something less mundane with her life immediately.

Coco trotted happily towards the bread, pleased he'd convinced her to correct her path. The figure became clearer as they got closer. He was young – an adult, but only just. Adeline guessed he'd died in the early 1900s, from the style of his suit and the cravat at his neck. Strangely, it made him look even younger and out of place – like a teenager forced into formal wear for a wedding, only playing at being a grown up.

Adeline hesitated. He was stepping backwards and forwards as if confused, his lips moving silently. This was unusual. Ghosts often had a set path they followed, but she'd never seen one pacing like this. She glanced down at Coco. He didn't seem worried, so she continued forward, picking up her loaf of bread.

"I don't know, I just don't know."

Adeline froze. She didn't turn around, but she knew there were no other shoppers close by. Coco's ears were pricked, having heard it too. She'd not heard a spirit speak before.

"It's not the same. None of it's the same."

The voice was whispery, and Adeline felt the chilling sensation of cold breath on the back of her neck.

"What do you want?" she choked out.

The figure behind her gasped. Adeline spun around, and the ghost's eyes widened, staring straight into Adeline's. They were face to face, close enough that Adeline could see he was made up of swirling smoke-like strands, just hinting at the outline of skin and clothes.

"You can hear me?" he asked.

Adeline frowned. The ghost seemed just as shocked as she was. His irises moved, twirling pools of grey and white. She could see fear in those eyes. No, not just fear... terror.

"What is it? What's wrong?" she asked him. Her voice dropped to a whisper, but the ghost wasn't listening. His gaze drifted away from her, seeming to stare at something just beside her. Adeline resisted the urge to turn and look, but goosebumps rose on that side of her neck as if a cold finger was trailing down her skin.

His figure became less clear, fading slowly into smoke and dissipating.

Adeline gave herself a moment for her heart rate to return to normal, then she shook her head. "That was a weird one, wasn't it?" she said to Coco. He wagged his tail agreeing with her. She turned to the shelf to grab her loaf of bread.

Coco growled. Adeline spun around and let out a little scream. The ghost had reappeared just inches from her face.

His hand darted out, grabbing her arm. "I'm sorry," he said.

"Don't!" Adeline tried to pull away, backing into the bread shelf. The dusty residue dislodged itself from her clothes, floating up into the air and making her cough.

Coils of smoke swirled off the ghost's hand and up over her skin. She jerked away, batting at the smoke to get it off, but it clung to her just like the dust had.

The ghost looked down, as surprised as she was.

Adeline gaped at him, unable to make sense of what he was doing. The smoke slid up over her, crawling towards her face. For a second, it seemed to take the shape of another person.

She shrieked, trying to bat it away, but the world was closing in. She heard Coco bark, felt him lean against her leg, aware that he would only do that if she were about to collapse. Smoke tendrils curled across her lips as if they would choke her.

"No!" she screamed.

The grey swirls clouded her vision. All she could hear was the ringing in her ears. And then there was nothing.

CHAPTER TWO

*A*deline woke to an ambulance officer leaning over her. She was on her side, Coco having pulled her over. He lay beside her now, guarding her. She felt his warm breath and a touch of drool on her neck. She shivered, remembering the cold puff of air that had hit her skin in exactly the same spot.

"Is the ghost still here?" she asked the ambulance officer, and instantly regretted it. She closed her eyes, trying to compose herself before speaking again.

A dream, she told herself. Or possibly a hallucination. It wasn't unusual for her to imagine things just before she lost consciousness. This had certainly been more vivid than normal, but it was probably just down to having seen two ghosts that day.

"Adeline... Adeline, can you open your eyes?"

He knew her name. She couldn't place him at this

moment, but something in the back of her mind recognised his voice. Thank goodness for small mercies! If it was an ambulance officer she'd met before, he would know her medical history and that she didn't need to go to the hospital. A cup of tea and a couple hours of sleep was usually all that was required when her body had one of its "uncooperative" days.

"Adeline..." She felt a hand on her collarbone and realised she still hadn't reopened her eyes.

She cracked her lids apart. "Oh..." She couldn't help the small sound escaping when she saw the warm, chocolatey brown eyes staring down at her. She sat up way too quickly, displacing Coco and making her head swim.

"Woah, easy now." He wrapped his arm around her before she ended up back on the ground.

She turned her face away, hiding behind the straggly bits of hair that had escaped her ponytail. All her relief at having someone she knew in attendance disappeared, knowing who it was. Hemi. He *was* an ambulance officer... but that wasn't where she knew him from.

"Always did like to be dramatic, didn't you, Adey?"

Adeline gave a strangled-sounding laugh, her cheeks flushing at the shortening of her name. He was the only one who'd ever called her that.

She scrabbled to sit up properly. "I'm fine. It wasn't a seizure, I just..." Her words disappeared in a puff of air. Coco leaned against her arm, pulling her back towards the ground.

Hemi chuckled. "Listen to your buddy, here. He's right – you need to lie down for a bit longer."

Adeline reluctantly agreed. Coco knew her better than anyone, and he wouldn't give an alert unless something was wrong. Hemi eased her back to lying flat, and Coco resumed his position guarding her.

"I'm fine, though," she told Hemi. "I just fainted. This isn't a big deal for me."

Hemi nodded, accepting that explanation without question. Usually, it would have been met with a bout of confused laughter, and an incredulous "What do you mean fainting isn't a big deal?!" or worse, a patronising "Really? Have you seen a doctor about that?" as if it wouldn't have occurred to her. Somehow, people couldn't quite get their heads around her having both epilepsy and low blood pressure. She guessed working for the ambulance service, Hemi had probably seen it all many times before. Besides, he'd been there when she'd had her first seizure, all those years ago.

Out of the corner of her eye, she saw the shop manager hovering, a form in his hands. An incident report, to add to the stack the store already had on file about her. She sighed. She wished she could get people to understand this was normal... well, normal for her, anyway.

The manager handed Hemi a bottle of water, which he opened and passed on to her. She would have to remember to pay for it before she left.

"Who called you?" she asked Hemi between sips. While

the shop staff had *kind of* gotten used to her malfunctioning body doing its own thing, members of the public tended to still overreact and call for help.

Hemi smiled. "No one." He gestured to an abandoned shopping basket. "I'm off duty. Just stopped in to get some stuff on my way home from work."

Adeline shook her head, ignoring the dizzy rush that gave her. *Very funny, Universe.* At least it was slightly better than finding out he was back in New Zealand during an actual medical emergency, though she wished they could have met on a day when she was wearing a bit of makeup or, at the very least, when she wasn't covered in attic-dust. He still looked exactly how she remembered him – his dark hair even sticking up in the same spot, and his grin making the familiar deep dimple appear on the right-hand side. She guessed she must look similar too, since he'd seemed to recognise her so easily.

When had he become a paramedic? she wondered, and how long had he been back in Wellington?

"You want to try sitting up again?"

Adeline nodded. She could feel her blood pressure coming right with the water. Hemi put his arm around her, and this time she reluctantly allowed herself to lean on him. Coco positioned himself next to her, ready to help stabilise her once she was on her feet.

"Have to say, never thought I'd find myself rescuing you, Adey."

Adeline couldn't see his face, but she could hear the

cheeky grin in his voice. She gave a snort in response. "You are *not* rescuing me."

"No?"

"No," she said firmly. Her head swum again as she turned to look at him, and she felt his hand tighten on her side, steadying her. "I'll concede you may, in fact, be helping me, though." She allowed herself a little smile as she met his eye.

He grinned back. "Everyone needs a little help sometimes."

Hemi offered to take her home. She wanted to say no – proudly tell him she could walk, but after a few steps her leg was shaking from the pain in her knee, and she wasn't confident she could make it without Coco having to help haul her up off the ground if her limbs gave way.

"Come on," Hemi said. "It'll give us a chance to catch up."

They paid for their groceries, the staff allowing them to queue-jump – an effort to get them out the door faster, she suspected – and headed out to the carpark. She smiled as he fell into a slow pace beside her. He didn't wrap his arm around her this time, instinctively understanding she didn't need it anymore, but he stayed close, just in case.

Even if he hadn't been leading the way, she would have known which car was his – a battered red mini with one white door, the same one he'd had since they were 17. He must have stored it with his parents while he was overseas.

Others might have upgraded as soon as they could, but she knew how much he loved that mini.

He held the door open for her, watching but not interfering as she negotiated getting her bung leg into the seat without bending it. Coco hopped in after her, curling up in the footwell and making himself comfortable.

"That is too cute," Hemi said. He took out his phone, snapping a quick picture of Coco's face leaning against the gear stick. "Where are we heading?"

"Tinakori Road," Adeline told him. She saw a flicker of recognition on his face, and her cheeks warmed. "Yeah... my parents' place."

Did he think it was weird she was still living in the same house she'd grown up in? The property had been in her family for generations, and it had made sense to stay, though she knew most 27-year-olds would have balked at the idea. All her high school friends had gone travelling, moved cities, or at the very least, gone flatting. That didn't usually worry her, but now she couldn't help wondering if Hemi thought her childish.

She shook her head. He'd been back in her life all of fifteen minutes, and she'd already flaked out on him twice. Her living in the same house was hardly going to be making the biggest impression.

"I was always jealous of your place growing up." He glanced at her. "Being able to walk into town seemed so much easier than catching the bus every day."

Not that she could walk that far at the moment, even when there weren't ghosts involved.

He stopped outside her door, by some miracle a carpark appearing right out front.

"Thank you," she said as she gathered her bag and Coco's lead. "For the lift, and for picking me up off the floor." Coco's tail flicked against her leg, excited at the prospect of being home.

"Of course. I'm glad it happened."

She shot him a look. "Um... really?" She tried to hold a frown, but laughter bubbled up as she saw an expression of horror cross his face.

"No! God, no, I'm not glad you collapsed. I just meant I'm glad I ran into you."

"It's okay. I knew what you meant." She put her hand on his, reassuring herself as much as him, but then she drew it back quickly, feeling awkward. Her palm tingled from the warmth of his skin, and she closed her fingers down over it.

He got out and walked up the steps with her. She had to take them one at a time, her knee protesting every bend. She certainly wouldn't be climbing the ladder to the roof again any time soon.

"It's good to see you." Hemi smiled, then his face went serious. He seemed unsure of himself, for the first time since she'd woken up in the shop. "I thought about getting in touch when I moved back, but..." He left it at that. She knew what he meant, though.

"But," she agreed. She'd thought about seeing if she could

get back in contact with him over the years, too. Somehow it had never quite happened. A sudden boldness overtook her. She slipped her phone out of her pocket. "Well, we better stay in touch this time." She unlocked the phone, adding his name and handing it over for him to write his number. He did the same, and she smiled when she saw he'd entered her name as "Adey".

"Adeline..." Hemi's hand brushed hers as he took his phone back.

She felt butterflies at his touch, but then grey tendrils slithered from her fingers, spreading up his arm. Adeline gasped. She blinked, hoping she was imagining things, but the smoke didn't clear. The colour drained from his face and something grey swirled over the surface of his eyes. Coils of it spiralled in his irises, obscuring the colour.

"Oh my god." She stepped back, the world swimming again.

Coco had frozen, staring up at the smoke, his tail alert. He wasn't growling, but Adeline felt like she wanted to growl herself. A protective instinct welled up inside her, yelling *Danger!*

"Are you okay?" Hemi's hand moved to her arm, and the smoke swarmed, detaching from her and swirling its way around him. A slither of it split off, snaking its way under the door and into the house. His skin was suddenly cold against hers.

Hemi swayed slightly, but he was still holding her arm, trying to steady her – trying to help *her* as she contaminated him with the smoke. Adeline shook herself, snapping out of her stupor and pushing Hemi away. The smoke disappeared as she did, and her breath came out in a rush.

"I'm fine," she told him. "But are you?" She peered into his face, tentatively touching his arm again, half expecting the smoke to reappear. Her heart rate relaxed a little when it didn't.

Hemi caught her hand. "I'm okay."

She heard the confusion in his voice. God, she must be making the strangest first impression. Though was it still a first impression when you'd known each other since you were teenagers?

She studied his face. His skin was still pale, and she could see a light sheen of sweat on his forehead. Her stomach twisted, wondering what exactly it was she had passed on to him. He was still holding her hand, and she withdrew it gently, not wanting to put him at further risk.

"I should go lie down." She gestured to the door, then shivered, thinking of the smoke creeping inside.

He nodded. "Get some rest. I'll text you later – check you haven't fallen out of bed. Wouldn't want to have to *rescue* you again." He grinned.

She nodded, only half listening as she found her keys. "Yeah… I mean no, I'll be fine. Coco will look after me." Coco wagged his tail at his name, his earlier tension gone. She opened the door, Coco following her inside.

Hemi raised his hand in a wave, which she returned. She

was disturbed to see her hand was shaking. She pushed the door closed before he saw.

As soon as the latch clicked into place, she wished she'd taken one last look at his eyes. Was the smoke still swirling inside them? She glanced back through the glass panel in her door, but he was gone.

CHAPTER THREE

*A*deline padded around the house in the evening, feeling again the emptiness of the space. The rooms had felt comfortable, when she was growing up, always filled with friends and neighbours dropping by, or her parents' laughter on quiet nights in. She didn't have aunts or uncles, nor any living grandparents, but she'd never felt the absence with all the other people in her parents' lives.

That absence was all too obvious now. She hadn't kept in touch with many of her parents' friends, finding it too awkward now her mum and dad were gone. The house had gotten quieter and quieter, the extra space expanding around her. Coco had helped fill some of it, since his arrival a year and a half ago, but the silence still got to Adeline sometimes.

Her mind kept wandering back to the moment on the doorstep, and she shuddered thinking of the swirling patterns in Hemi's eyes. She couldn't see any signs of the smoke that had crept under the door. Had she imagined it, or was it in here, lurking somewhere? The thought made the empty rooms even more daunting.

Adeline jumped as her phone beeped. She picked it up, her stomach fluttering a little as she saw it was a text from Hemi.

Still conscious? it read.

She started typing out a reply, then stopped, unsure of what to say. She tried again, but nothing she wrote felt quite funny or clever enough to send. Maybe she shouldn't reply tonight, pretend she was asleep and reply in the morning. She put the phone down, and went to the bathroom, giving herself a moment to think.

Coco followed her, seeming to think she needed company in there. She didn't, of course, but at least the humour of that distracted her a little.

She returned to the living room, Coco trotting along behind her, and picked up her phone again. Had it been too long to reply now? She knew if people took too long to answer her messages, she'd often forgotten about the conversation, having moved on to do something else instead.

Adeline stopped, taking a breath. This overthinking was exactly why she was lonely. She sent Hemi a cat and a tree emoji with the words: *Still conscious. You'll have to find a cat stuck in a tree to rescue instead.*

He sent back a crying-laughing emoji, and it went on like that for a while. Suddenly she was sixteen again, staying up late, messaging a boy. Then she remembered the chill on his hand and the way the smoke had spread up his arm when she touched him. Whatever the ghost had done to her, she had passed it on to him. She couldn't bear the idea she might have hurt him.

She ended the conversation, telling him she was going to bed. In reality, she sat up half the night, unable to sleep.

Adeline still felt unsettled in the morning, but she couldn't work out if that was from having fainted, or from the rest of it.

In all her years of seeing ghosts, one had never spoken to her, and she'd certainly never seen one attach to a living person like that. If she hadn't seen the smoke in Hemi's eyes, perhaps she could have gone on believing it was just an effect of her low blood pressure, but now?

She decided to take Coco down to the park before work. There were usually a few other dogs around, so he could get some exercise, playing, without her having to tax her sore knee too much. Besides, she enjoyed the peaceful atmosphere of sitting beside the park's reflection pool. It was in memory of Katherine Mansfield, but Adeline had never seen the author there. She'd never seen *any* ghosts in the park, which was exactly what she wanted today.

She took Coco's jacket off when they reached the grass. "Go free," she said, and he bounded off, doing a loop around the park before returning to her with a stick in his mouth. "Good boy! Good boy, Coco."

He froze suddenly, tail straight up and ears alert.

"It's okay, puppy," she said to him, but he kept staring. She turned around, expecting to see a cat, or perhaps just a plastic bag that looked like one. Instead, she jumped, finding a woman sitting on the bench behind her, a black Labrador beside her. The former was probably in her forties and had long red hair, swept over one shoulder. She wore a fifties-style black dress and cat's eye sunglasses with little diamantes in the corners. The look was striking, and Adeline wondered how she could have missed spotting the woman. Somehow, she'd managed to blend into the leafy background.

"I'm sorry, I didn't see you there."

The woman gave a half laugh. "Naturally, I didn't see you at all."

It was then that Adeline noticed the harness on the dog. "Oh, she's working." She took hold of Coco's collar to stop him approaching the guide dog. "Sit," she told him. "You can't play while she's on duty."

The woman smiled, probably in relief that she didn't have to explain the rules – Adeline knew that feeling.

"I was just about to let her off." The woman reached

over, feeling along the harness until she found the clip. "Off you go, Lola," she said as she released it. "Go play."

The two dogs dashed towards each other, pausing to sniff and check each other out, then Lola dipped her shoulders in a play bow, and Coco followed suit. They were off, racing up the slope on the other side of the park.

The woman patted the bench next to her.

Adeline felt awkward but sat down, nonetheless. "I haven't seen you here before," she said. There were a crowd of human and dog pairs she and Coco saw regularly on their walks. Coco was much more social then she was though. Adeline knew most of the dog's names, but next to none of their human counterparts.

"I don't normally come this way, but Lola told me we should today."

"I know what you mean." Adeline laughed, thinking of Coco yesterday when she tried to skip buying bread. "Coco's an assistance dog too," she added, when she realised the woman wouldn't have seen his vest, even before she'd taken it off.

"Oh, I know." A small smile played at the corners of the woman's lips.

Adeline opened her mouth but then shut it again before she thought of anything to say. Had they met before? Adeline didn't think so. The woman's style was so distinctive, Adeline was sure she would have remembered. Besides, she had a very good memory for dogs, and she definitely would have recognised Lola.

She glanced across the park to where Coco and Lola sat quietly side by side on the slope, looking out over the park. That was unusual. Normally, Coco would be racing around the park, encouraging any other dogs to play chase, or rolling in the grass, a stick in his mouth. Instead, the two of them just sat, as if deep in conversation.

"Lola said you would be here," the woman said.

Adeline blinked, tearing her eyes away from the dogs. "Huh?"

"She told me there was another familiar she needed to connect with."

Adeline nodded, then changed her mind and shook her head, realising too late the woman couldn't see either gesture. "I'm sorry, what?"

The woman laughed, lightly. "Oh goodness, you have no idea, do you?" She reached out, placing her hand on Adeline's arm.

Adeline went to pull away, but then stopped, her eyes going wide. Coils of something orange were spreading up Adeline's arm from the woman's hand. They moved in the same way the smoke from the ghost had, but it wasn't cold this time. The woman's hand was warm, and the sensation spread through Adeline, calming her.

"What *is* this?" she whispered. She could hear a little panic in her voice, despite the soothing feeling of the glow.

The woman didn't answer, seemingly deep in concentration. The tips of her fingers tapped a gentle rhythm on Adeline's skin. "There," she said finally. "Now you know."

"Know what?" But even as the words left her mouth, Adeline realised she *did* know. Suddenly, it was like there was a map of the city spreading out in Adeline's mind. She couldn't *see* it exactly; it was more like she could sense lines of static electricity stretching out around her. All along them, she could feel little threads marking the path to other people and other animals... no, not animals, *familiars.*

Familiars, she said the word in her mind, testing it out. She'd always imagined them as cats in stories – black cats specifically – sitting perched on the back of witch's broomsticks as they went about their witchy business. The animals she could sense along the threads weren't like that at all, but somehow the term still felt right.

As she touched each thread, she felt information about the person and familiar it connected to rushing into her mind. She found Lola, and in a breath, it was like she had known the woman next to her all their lives.

"Clara?" she asked.

The woman nodded. "That's me."

She tried to follow another of the threads, but it disintegrated before she could reach the end.

Clara drew back her hand. "It's too much information to take in all at once, especially when your other senses are fighting for attention. That's why it's easier for me." She touched her sunglasses as if gesturing to her blindness.

Adeline could understand that. Feeling all the strands on top of seeing and hearing everything in the park in front of her had been dizzying. Like trying to read a text while jogging.

Adeline rubbed her temples, clearing the remains of the effect. "What *was* that?" She searched for all the knowledge she'd had just a moment before, but it had disappeared when Clara let go.

Clara frowned. "Your family didn't teach you any of this?"

Adeline shook her head. "My parents died when I was eighteen." She wasn't sure it would have made a difference, even if they had still been here. They had both been absolutely baffled by her talk of ghosts, blaming it on her seizures, though Adeline was sure it wasn't related. Eventually, she'd just stopped mentioning it.

Coco came to her side, gently nudging her hand. Adeline felt her heart rate slow in response. She stroked his head, letting him calm her.

"Well, it's a very good thing Coco found you, in that case. I hate to think what would have happened to your magic otherwise."

"My magic?"

Coco moved from nudging to licking, as Adeline's pulse spiked again. Strangely, it wasn't with fear, or even confusion, but something else. Excitement. It was like a part of her mind had just opened up, and suddenly her life was starting to make so much more sense. She'd never thought of it as magic, but she had always seen things – known things – that she shouldn't have been able to. And now that she considered it, she had started seeing more spirits since Coco had been placed with her. They'd become more solid too, though yesterday was the first time she'd seen anything as intense as the ghost in the supermarket.

Clara didn't answer her question, perhaps realising Adeline was slowly figuring it out on her own.

"If you don't come from a magical family..." Clara hesitated. "You're not adopted, are you?"

"No... at least I don't think so." Adeline felt a sudden panic at not being able to ask her parents. Was it possible they weren't biologically related? Then their faces swum into her mind and she shook her head. "No, definitely not. I look exactly like my parents."

"Wilson's a very common surname. I won't be able to track the magic that way."

Adeline froze. How did Clara know her surname? Then again, Adeline knew Clara's name without having been told it. The magical knowledge must work both ways. Still, it made her uneasy.

Clara traced a hand in the air as if following one of the threads she'd shown Adeline earlier. "Dunningham," she mumbled to herself.

Adeline shivered at the mention of her mother's maiden name.

Clara's hand paused in the air. "It's possible that maybe..." She trailed off.

"What? What is it?"

Clara turned to her. "Do you have access to a family tree?"

Adeline started to shake her head, but then stopped herself. "Maybe. I think I might have one. My mum's side of the family. I remember seeing it in a box of old photos. Why?" If Clara could track her family history through invisible lines in the air, what difference would a family tree make?

"I'm not sure," Clara said, but it was almost like she was having a conversation with herself. "There's something odd here... I should be able to see further back."

"Odd how?"

"I don't know, I can't quite explain it, there's just some kind of block. But it's important. Find the tree as soon as you can."

Adeline shifted, uncomfortable with being given directives by a stranger, especially such weird ones. How could this woman possibly know that a piece of paper she'd never seen – that Adeline had barely seen herself – was important? She glanced sideways at Clara. Was she being ridiculous accepting her word that Coco was a familiar? The more Adeline let herself think about it, the more doubts started to creep in.

Clara's mouth tightened, perhaps sensing Adeline's hesitation. "I'm sorry," she said. "This must be a lot for you."

Adeline gave a short laugh. "You could say that."

Clara's expression showed an internal argument. Adeline wasn't sure which side was winning, but eventually, the older woman sighed. "I don't mean to rush or frighten you, it's just there's something coming. I can feel the energy of it all over you."

Without meaning to, Adeline's hand moved to the place on her arm, where the ghost had grabbed her. She thought again of the grey swirls that had covered Hemi, and the way they had coiled out from her skin. Was that what Clara meant?

"No wonder Lola said we had to meet you," Clara added.

Adeline glanced at the guide dog, confused. Did she mean Lola literally spoke to her? No – Adeline thought of the times Coco alerted her to a coming seizure or reminded her of the way home when she was confused after one. He didn't need words to communicate. But there were other times too, like when he insistently pulled her somewhere or seemed to know before she did where they were going.

"Does Lola do that often? Tell you things, I mean," she asked.

"Only when there's something important."

Coco had encouraged her to go to the bread aisle yesterday. Had he wanted her to see the ghost? That didn't seem right – he had growled when it grabbed her.

"Something happened yesterday," she told Clara.

"What kind of something?"

Adeline let out a breath, unsure how she could possibly explain. "It's complicated."

"May I?" Clara held out her hand.

Adeline hesitated, and Clara's face softened. "Just take

my hand and think about what happened. I'll be able to glean what I need to know."

Adeline couldn't help but feel sceptical of that, but she'd gotten this far – what could it hurt? She felt silly holding hands but did as she was told anyway. She thought about the ghost, mentally running through everything that had happened, right up until the smoke had swirled around Hemi and slipped under her door. She tried to break off the memory there, but she had a feeling Clara still knew she was thinking about the cutesy text exchange she'd had with him later. Of all the things to focus on, her brain had to get stuck on that!

"Hmm..." Clara said eventually. "The ghost's name is Stanley. I don't see spirits myself, but I've heard about him from others who do. He died there in 1910. Harmless, but you're right, it's very unusual for him to be able to interact with you like that."

Adeline shivered. The idea of someone dying in the supermarket creeped her out immensely. Perhaps that was why the store manager was always so quick to make her fill out an incident report every time she had a seizure. Adeline frowned. Would the shop have been there in 1910? No, that didn't seem right. She had a vague memory of her father telling her what it used to be. A brewery, maybe. She remembered him saying something about how it used to heat the swimming pool. She would have to look it up when she got home.

"That energy he had around him... it wasn't from him; it

was something else." Clara tilted her head as if listening. "It's not attached to your friend anymore either."

The knot in Adeline's stomach relaxed, her relief that Hemi wasn't being hurt by it immeasurable.

"But it's still moving," Clara continued. "Passing from person to person. I think that's what he wanted from you – to use you as a link to others."

The knot tightened up again at that. "Is it dangerous?" What had she exposed Hemi to? She'd been back in his life for all of five minutes and had already introduced a super-natural threat to their friendship. And to think she'd been embarrassed about fainting in front of him!

Clara made a noise in her throat. "Not by itself. It will just depend who it reaches." She tilted her head as if she were listening to something. "It's hard for me to track it when it's passing through so many people though. There are too many threads."

That was the weird thing about living in a place like Wellington. There were only two degrees of separation between people, so if the energy was hopping between them, it wouldn't be long until it had reached the entire population. Besides, what did that mean about the smoke that had crept under her door into her house? She hadn't seen any further signs of it, but that didn't mean it wasn't still there somewhere, lurking.

Clara stood, and Lola bounded across the park, rushing to her side. Clara clipped the harness back into place, and

Lola's demeanour changed instantly to serious focus, just like Coco's did when Adeline put his vest on.

Adeline stood too. "I... There's so much more I need to ask you." A small part of her felt strange that she was accepting everything, but somehow it all felt right. She felt freer – more complete – than she had in a long time.

"I know, and there will be time for that, but right now, we both need to get to work."

Adeline blinked. Clara was correct, she was already running late for the office, but the idea of going back to normality after she had just found out she was a... Adeline came up short. "If Coco's a familiar, does that make me a..."

"Witch. Yes, that's what you are," Clara said, matter-of-factly.

Adeline made a small sound, that wasn't quite a word. She swallowed and tried again. "Okay, then," was all she managed, and then she started to laugh.

Clara smiled at her in a somewhat bemused way. Adeline wouldn't be surprised if she thought she was becoming a little unhinged – a part of her was wondering that herself. But she didn't seem offended by Adeline's laughter, at least.

"We'll meet again soon, but first you need to look for that family tree, and I need to follow up some other threads."

"Yes, okay, I will find it." Adeline's laughter petered out. Having a specific task to do helped, even if it was a bizarre one. She would find the box of photos after work.

"Coco and Lola will arrange a time for us to meet."

Adeline let out another little giggle at that. It was like their assistance dogs – their *familiars* – were secretaries, scheduling meetings for them.

Clara picked up her bag, turning towards the park entrance. "And Adeline? Let go of that guilt." A little smile tweaked her lips. "I have a suspicion you'll be hearing from Hemi again very soon."

CHAPTER FOUR

*A*deline opened yet another drawer and sighed at the stack of papers inside. She'd already known she wasn't the world's tidiest person, but searching through all the nooks and crannies of the house, looking for the family tree and photographs, had made her question how she ever got a job as an office manager. At work, she knew exactly where everything was, careful filing and storage systems meaning finding something was as simple as reaching for it. At home, it seemed like she was going to have to conduct an archaeological dig to wade down through all the bits and pieces she and her parents had collected over the years.

Despite her systems, Adeline had gotten barely anything done at work that day. Spreadsheets swum in front of her eyes, when she was at her desk, and more than once she had to ask for clarification when writing minutes for meetings.

She'd noticed her boss glancing at her, his concern evident, but everyone in the office knew that they only had to be worried if Coco was. He'd stayed firmly asleep under the desk, using her feet as a pillow and letting out little snores every so often.

Adeline was a pretty conscientious worker, and usually finished whatever task she was doing before leaving the office, but today she'd been out the door as soon as the clock hit 5 p.m.

She opened another cupboard and began sorting through the boxes inside. Coco lay in the doorway, watching. He often did this if she wasn't settled in the living room in the evenings. She figured sleeping across the doorway was his way of making sure she didn't go anywhere unexpected without him.

Adeline shifted another box and found her mother's sewing stuff behind it. She took the basket out, imagining she could smell her mother's perfume wafting from the fabric inside. In reality, all she could smell was dust. Something tugged at her memory as she examined the quilted lid. It was bigger than she remembered and didn't fit the picture she had in her mind of her mother opening a blue box looking for a needle and thread. This basket did seem familiar, though, but the memory wouldn't quite unfold.

As interesting as it was, sewing supplies were not what she was looking for. If Clara was right, and there really was some force coming, she needed to focus. How her family tree and some old photographs would help, she couldn't imagine, but she wouldn't figure it out unless she found them. She placed the basket on the floor, mentally telling herself she would allow herself to sort through it once she'd located the box she needed.

Coco sat up, giving a big stretch. She glanced at him.

"What's wrong, puppy?" she asked. "Do you need to go out?" Usually, if he needed to go, his ears would pop up at the mention of the word "out". This time they stayed flat.

"It's not dinner time yet," she told him. *Labradors and their stomachs*, she thought to herself.

But that didn't seem to be it either. Coco moved over to her, lying next to the sewing basket and giving a big sigh. Adeline frowned. Clara had said that Lola told her things, but you had to know how to listen. Was this Coco's way of trying to tell her something?

She picked up the sewing basket, and Coco leapt up, tail wagging. He trotted down the hallway to the living room, glancing back to check whether she was following. Adeline did, taking the sewing supplies with her. She wasn't sure what she was supposed to do with them, but Clara had said to pay attention to Coco. If he was a familiar, he must have some powers she didn't, including being able to tell what was important.

Adeline sat down on the couch, and Coco plonked himself on her feet, keeping her in place. The lid of the basket was made of green patchwork fabric, with a braided wicker edge. The basket itself was octagonal shaped and lined with more of the green, floral patterned fabric inside.

Little pockets and compartments were sewn into the lining, to keep different supplies separate. Adeline touched the pockets gently. She remembered her mother showing her how to sew when she was small. This wasn't her mum's sewing box, it was her grandmother's, or great grandmother's... possibly even further back. In her mind, she saw her mother's hands, spending hours picking up thread and turning over pieces of fabric to show her. She could almost hear her mother's voice telling her things about each, but the words were tantalisingly just out of reach.

Adeline closed her eyes, letting the memories wash over her. When she opened them, the hands she'd seen in her mind were still there. She gasped, looking up. A ghost sat next to her, reaching over to sort through the fabric in Adeline's lap. It wasn't her mother, but the resemblance was strong. She had the same straight, narrow nose, the same tilt to her head, and one deep wrinkle on the right-hand side, from the lopsided frown that appeared when she was nervous.

The ghost looked up, smiling at Adeline. Adeline forced her mouth into a wobbly return smile. Was this her great-grandmother? Great-great-grandmother, even? Adeline's heart was fluttering painfully in her chest. She'd never seen the ghost of someone related to her before; she'd not even been sure it was possible. A part of her wanted to scan the room, desperately hoping her mother was about to appear too, but her eyes remained glued to the spirit beside her, not fully trusting her after what had happened in the supermarket.

The woman reached out, as if she were going to take something from the box, but then her face suddenly distorted, the smoke swirling away, like someone had swatted their hand through it.

Adeline felt cold. She stood up, still clutching the sewing box in her hands. "Hello?" she called. "Are you still here? Can you hear me?"

All the lights in the room flickered, a coil of smoke circling the bulb in the centre of the ceiling. She heard a loud screeching noise, like an old tap turning on.

"Hello?" she tried again.

Coco began to whine, a low growl starting in his throat. This was not her grandmother. Whatever this was, it was not friendly. The house began to shake. Before Adeline could drop to the ground, the sewing box flew out of her hands, shooting across the room, and knocking Adeline's glass of water from the table, shattering it. She screamed, throwing herself to the ground, covering her own and Coco's head with her arms. The shaking increased, rumbling as if hundreds of pairs of hands were beating against the walls and windows. She heard things crash around her, and one of the windows exploded, sending more glass showering over her.

Drop, cover, hold, she said in her mind, repeating the phrase like a mantra. "Drop, cover, hold," she said aloud, not knowing why, but suddenly feeling compelled to do so. "Drop, cover, hold!" she screamed.

The shaking stopped. She held her position for a moment, before risking a peek out. She glanced around the room but couldn't see any sign of the smoke. Coco sat up, licking her face frantically.

"Good boy," she said, her voice hoarse and wobbly. "Good boy."

Coco continued licking, and she stroked his head, trying to calm both of them.

There was a knock on the door. Adeline let out another scream, which she cut short when she realised where the sound was coming from.

"Adeline? Adey, are you okay?"

She recognised Hemi's voice and pulled herself up, wincing as she straightened her knee. She'd knocked it yet again on the way down, probably undoing any progress she'd made in its healing.

"Adey!"

She heard the panic in Hemi's voice and limped to the door. What was he doing here? She mentally ran through the conversation they'd had the night before, wondering if she'd overlooked something. Coco rushed ahead of her, the shaking forgotten in his excitement to greet someone. She opened the door, and Coco changed his mind, rushing off to get a toy to present Hemi with instead.

Hemi stepped inside without waiting for an invitation. The light from the street behind him gave him a soft, green aura, but there was no sign of the smoke around him. He moved toward her, wrapping her in a hug. "Oh my god, Adey, I heard you scream, are you okay?"

Adeline waited for him to take a breath before nodding into his shoulder. "I'm okay, I'm okay. Are you?"

"Yeah." He took another breath and she heard it shudder as he released it.

They held each other for a moment, both needing the stability. Adeline closed her eyes and finally felt her heart rate start to slow. Coco returned and squeezed himself between their legs, his tail bashing both of them as it waved back and forth causing his whole rear end to dance.

Hemi pulled back, but his hand stayed resting on Adeline's arm. "Hey, buddy," he said to Coco. He went to pat him, then hesitated and gave Adeline a questioning look.

"Yeah, you can play with him. His vest is off, so he's off duty."

Hemi dropped down into a crouch, and Coco danced excitedly on the spot, pressing the toy towards Hemi's face. "Good boy. Aren't you a good boy?" He glanced up at Adeline in between pats. "Are you sure you're okay? Is anything broken?"

"I don't know. Yes," she said, remembering the crashes. "The window." She glanced around the house, noticing the dim light. "I think the power might be out. I have some candles."

Hemi made a noise in his throat. "Probably not a good idea. There might be aftershocks. Do you have a torch?"

"Maybe. I don't know." She had an earthquake kit, but her mind was blanking on where.

"There's one in my car. Stay inside, I'll go get it."

Adeline walked back into the living room as Hemi rushed outside. Should she be letting him do that? It seemed a big risk to go running out straight after a quake – everything she'd ever been taught told her they should stay put, but she had a suspicion this hadn't been a normal seismic event.

She didn't venture too far into the room, as her feet were bare, and she knew there would be smashed glass covering the floor. Hemi returned quickly with the torch and a bag from his car.

He shone the beam around. "Woah, don't move. There's glass everywhere."

Adeline had already frozen. By some miracle, she had managed not to stand on any, but the shards glinted all around her as the torch beam hit them. She eyed the glass, searching for a path through, then took a tentative step forward.

"Ow!" She winced as a splinter dug into her foot.

"What are you doing? Seriously, Adey, stay where you are." Hemi grabbed her hand, helping her balance as she pulled the sliver of glass from her foot, a drop of blood oozing out in its place.

"Yeah, okay, you're right." Her stomach tightened as she thought of Coco. "Can you shut Coco in the hallway?"

Hemi moved quickly, doing exactly as she asked. Coco

looked miserable at being separated from her, but at least his paws would be safe.

"Do you have a dustpan?" Hemi called.

"Under the sink in the kitchen. And could you please grab my slippers from upstairs?" She was not thrilled about the thought of sending him up to her bedroom, which she knew looked like the wardrobe had vomited all over the floor, but she didn't have another option. "Second door on the right. But you're still not rescuing me," she called after him. She heard him bark out a laugh in response.

Hemi returned with the slippers and a band aid. He took her hand again, helping her balance while she tended to her foot.

"Don't you dare comment on the state of my room."

He laughed again. "Don't worry, mine looks the same... minus the bra on the doorknob."

Oh god, she didn't even know if he was joking. She had a habit of flinging off her bra as soon as she got home from work, and it wouldn't be out of character for her to have left it hanging somewhere strange. She couldn't even remember which one she'd been wearing that day, but the way things had been going with Hemi, chances are it would be the Ninja Turtle one she'd bought on sale because it was so comfortable and just so weird she had to have it.

"You try wearing one of those all day," she said after an awkwardly long pause. "You'd be throwing it across the room too."

He chuckled. "Fair enough."

She took the dustpan from him, moving carefully even with the slippers protecting her feet. Hemi held the torch low to the ground so she could sweep up the shards.

"Reckon that was a magnitude 4 or 5? Not the biggest I've ever felt, but it was a pretty strong jolt."

Adeline nodded. "Yeah, about that." She felt like she was producing at least a 2.1 by herself with the trembling in her hands. The dustpan shook, sending some of the glass clattering back to the floor.

"Let me do that." Hemi reached for the dustpan.

Adeline pulled it away. "No, I'm fine, I can do it." But her hands were still shaking, and there was next to nothing left in the pan now.

"Hey." Hemi took the brush from her. "It's okay, I got this. Go sit down."

She wanted to protest, but her chest was squeezing tight making the tremors worse. She nodded, letting him take over the clean-up as she made her way to the couch, checking for glass on the cushions before sitting. She felt calmer as soon as she was off her feet. Calmer still when Hemi finished picking up the broken glass, and let Coco back into the room, both of them coming to sit on the couch beside her.

She stroked Coco's head, noting his relaxed posture as he leaned against her. *There's nothing to worry about now*, he seemed to say. And somehow, she knew he was right. The energy in the room had changed as soon as she had shouted those words, and now Hemi and Coco were beside her, she felt a placidness replacing the frenetic tension the earthquake had caused.

She glanced at Hemi, wondering how he could have that effect. He rubbed his face, and she was surprised to see he was shaking too.

"Hey." She took his hands between hers, squeezing them gently. "Are *you* okay?"

"Yeah, yeah, I'm fine." His words were light, but there was a wobble in his voice.

Adeline pulled him back into a hug. "It's okay if you're not."

He laughed. "True, I guess I'm not. I've been overseas a long time. I forgot what earthquakes feel like."

Adeline nodded. Even having lived in Wellington the whole time, with jolts a fairly regular occurrence, they still had the power to get the adrenaline racing. She pulled back from the hug, rubbing Hemi's shoulder as she did. "You'll feel better after some food. Come help me get the power back on, and I'll make you some dinner."

The fuse box was too high for Adeline to reach, so she dragged a chair into the hallway and climbed up on it, sucking in a deep breath as her knee protested.

Hemi leant against the wall, his arms folded as he watched her. "You know, I could have reached that if you'd let me," he said.

It was true. He was tall enough he wouldn't have even needed a chair. Or rather, he was average-heighted enough to not need a chair. Adeline sometimes forgot the rest of the population had at least half a foot on her.

"Where's the fun in that? Besides, I need you to hold the torch." She located the tripped fuse and reset it, allowing herself a satisfied smile when the living room lights came back on.

Then she looked down at the ground, realising she hadn't quite thought this through.

"Need a hand to get down?" A laugh hinted at the corners of Hemi's mouth.

Adeline considered jumping then thought better of it. "Yes, please." She waited for him to make another joke about rescuing her, but he held his tongue, perhaps realising the offer of dinner might be conditional on him not pissing her off.

He helped her down, then she fed Coco and they made their way to the kitchen.

"Vegetable bake okay with you?" *It better be,* she added to herself, as she didn't have the ingredients for anything else.

Hemi grinned. "As long as there's lots of cheese in it."

"Naturally." Adeline had a vague memory of a group of friends coming over during the school holidays once and making something similar for them. Had Hemi been there? She couldn't remember, but he probably would have been. He'd been one of her best friends all through high school.

She opened the cupboard, taking out an onion and a

couple of cloves of garlic. She handed them to Hemi. "Chopping board's over there."

He raised his eyebrows. "Oh, so when you said you'd make me dinner, you really meant you'd put me to work?"

"Gotta pay your way, buddy." She bumped him with her hip on her way past.

"I see Coco doesn't have to work for his dinner."

Coco had finished his meal and was now sitting in the doorway giving his best hungry look, in the hopes Hemi might be fooled into giving him more.

"Coco's been working all day, thank you very much. Takes a lot of effort monitoring my wonky body."

Coco wagged his tail, recognising she was talking about him.

Hemi chuckled. "I think your body is doing just fine."

Adeline turned away as she blushed. She was sure he didn't mean that how it had sounded, but it made her self-conscious anyway. She busied herself with grating cheese – lots, as per his request.

"Were you on your way home from work?" she asked.

Hemi nodded. "Yeah, I was driving past, and I thought I'd drop by, see if you were home. I was just about to knock when the shaking started."

Adeline blushed again. Delight filled her, at the idea that him just "dropping by" might become a regular thing. Suddenly, she felt sixteen again, crushing hard on her best friend.

"That was nice of you," she said. It sounded silly and

prim, but she was finding herself tongue tied. She jumped as she felt his hand on her side.

He leaned over her, reaching for some cheese. "I wanted to see you again," he said.

She looked up at him. He held her eye, and she forced herself to return his gaze. He popped the cheese in his mouth but didn't step back. Normally, in situations like this, she would tie herself in mental knots, convincing herself that the person wasn't flirting with her – or if she couldn't convince herself of that, then she'd tell herself she didn't want them to be. But this was Hemi. Of course she wanted him to be flirting with her.

Adeline swallowed. "I wanted to see you again too."

He grinned, grabbing another handful of cheese. "The cooking is just a bonus."

She laughed, her nervous tension finally easing. "Wait 'til you taste it before you say that."

CHAPTER FIVE

*H*emi helped her board up the smashed window after dinner, but she didn't pick up the sewing box, letting it lie on the floor where it had landed. It wasn't that she was afraid, exactly, just she didn't want a repeat of the earthquake – or whatever it was – while Hemi was there. She couldn't let herself think about the power behind what had happened.

They sat on the couch chatting, instead, Coco asleep between them. The food made them both feel better, exactly as Adeline had said it would. A part of her wondered if there was some magic in that. Now Clara had brought it up, she was seeing magic in everything. There had definitely been some power in the words she'd yelled during the earthquake. Were magic words a real thing? Yet another question to add to her list for Clara.

Hemi told her about his travels. She found she wasn't

jealous, like she usually was when people told her about their lives, and all the things she would probably never get to experience herself. Instead, she listened, rapt, as she lived vicariously through his adventures.

He asked what she'd been up to while he'd been gone, and about Coco. He laughed at her stories, and she found her life didn't seem quite so boring when she had an audience who found her entertaining. Soon they were both giggling without even knowing why, just like they had as teenagers.

She'd missed this. The warmth of having someone in her space – those tingly nice moments of contact when his arm brushed against hers patting Coco, or he grabbed her hand when gesturing mid-story. More than that, she'd missed the life having another person there brought to the room.

Eventually, they both started to yawn, and she sent him home. Or at least she started to. They ended up standing on her doorstep, talking and giggling some more. When he finally turned to leave, she saw a flicker of something in his face. The way his lips parted, and his eyes dropped to look at hers, she thought he might be about to kiss her. But then he frowned slightly and gave her a hug instead. She couldn't help but feel a little disappointed at that.

Adeline was still yawning at her desk the next day. Hemi had left just after ten, but she hadn't been able to sleep. She knew she should have continued her search for the family tree, but she hadn't done that, opting to lie awake thinking about it instead. She didn't pick up the sewing box again either. Perhaps she *was* a little afraid, if she was honest with herself.

She knew she would have to find it – to face reality – eventually, especially if the energy that had been attached to her and Hemi continued to spread. The smoke hadn't shown up in the house again, since the earthquake, but she still wondered what it was doing there in the first place. Clara had said the energy was probably just using her as a link to pass from person to person, but then why was some of it lingering around her house? And why had it objected to her looking at a sewing box of all things?

She wished she'd insisted on getting Clara's phone number. Waiting for her and Lola to come find them seemed like a faulty way of doing things with so much going on.

Faulty... fault lines... Adeline shook her head. She must be tired. She was laughing at her own terrible puns.

"Late night, was it?" One of her co-workers, Dana, grinned at her from across the office as Adeline yawned yet again.

As Adeline's eyes refocused, Dana seemed to have a warm, orange glow around her. Adeline blinked, trying to make it clear, but it didn't. Adeline's heart rate sped up, anxiety and excitement fighting for her attention at this new, potentially magical, phenomenon. The colour fitted

Dana's personality, Adeline thought – bubbly and cosy. She took a breath, letting the excitement win.

"Just couldn't sleep after the earthquake," she told Dana.

"Didn't feel it. What time was it?"

Adeline frowned. The shaking had been strong enough that she'd thought everyone would have felt it, or at the very least have heard about it. "About five-thirty, I think? My power went out too."

"Weird, I didn't feel a thing."

Adeline glanced around the office. A few people had headphones in, but most were listening in on their conversation – the joys of open plan offices. "You all felt it right?"

She was met with shakes of the head, mumbled but very unsure "maybes". No one seemed to have experienced the same thing she had.

"Wow," she said finally. Hemi had definitely felt it, as had Coco. Was it possible for an earthquake to be that localised? She pulled Geonet up on her screen, checking through the usual list of small quakes from the day before. There was nothing mentioned that would account for what she and Hemi had felt.

"Maybe it's that old house of yours?" Dana offered.

Adeline found herself nodding, though she didn't believe it. "Must be that."

Adeline decided to head to the park again on her lunch break. Partly to give Coco a chance to run around, and partly in the hope that she would find Clara and Lola waiting for them. On the way there, she couldn't help noticing the colours surrounding people she passed. She had never believed in auras, she'd always assumed it was just a trick of the light, or people's eyesight deteriorating. But suddenly everyone seemed to have one.

She blinked, trying to clear it by focusing her eyes, but she already knew it wasn't that. The colours seemed to fit the nature of the people she passed. Not that she knew them, of course, but it was like their personalities were spilling out into spectrums of light, inviting her to know more.

She smiled at people, and she noticed their auras seemed to warm as she did. The ones with orange light around them most often smiled back, their energy seeming just as infectiously happy as Dana's.

There was that word again – energy.

There was something else she noticed, but she didn't really want to acknowledge it. Every so often, out of the corner of her eye, she'd see someone surrounded not just with colour, but with smoke. It would only ever be around one person, and when she turned to look, it would be gone. She hoped she was imagining it, mistaking cigarettes or vapes for the supernatural signature, but when she saw two people bump into each other at a corner, and the smoke pass from one to the other as they said their apologies, she knew that was wishful thinking.

Coco was pulling slightly on the lead, pressing her to walk faster than she would have liked with her sore knee. He sometimes did this when she wasn't feeling well, as if trying to keep up her momentum and encourage her to keep moving, so she didn't pay much attention at first. Then suddenly, he veered to the right.

"Straight on, Coco," she called, but he didn't look at her, pulling again instead.

Adeline looked up. They were outside an antique shop, and Coco was trying to take her down a path leading around the back of it. She sighed. Clara had said to trust him, but this could get embarrassing if he turned out to just be following a scent, and she was caught wandering onto someone else's property.

Coco looked up at her, his tail wagging, and then pointedly turned to look down the path, giving a slight tug on his lead.

"Okay, puppy. Let's go have a look."

Coco trotted along, happy now Adeline was following. They came to a door, a small wooden sign reading "Witch Way" above it.

"I had no idea this was here," she told Coco. He wagged his tail in response.

Witch Way... That couldn't be a coincidence. Adeline hesitated. She had an odd feeling of trespassing. Clara had told her she was a witch, but it didn't feel like her world yet.

She looked down at Coco. He'd brought her here, but he didn't appear to be in a hurry to approach the door. He stared back at her, seemingly quite content with just standing outside.

Adeline took one step towards the door, still debating whether she had the courage to go inside. But before she reached it, the door opened, a bell jangling and making her jump as it did.

A black, wet nose appeared and headed straight for Coco.

"Clara!" Adeline burst out, as Lola pulled Clara towards her. "You have no idea how glad I am to see you!"

Clara stepped back, startled, and Adeline realised immediately that she should have announced herself, or at least said hello before launching in.

"I'm sorry," she said. "I thought you knew I was here."

Clara pressed a hand to her chest, calming herself. "Unfortunately, magical senses don't always make up for the missing ordinary ones."

"Of course. I'm sorry."

Clara smiled, easing Adeline's guilt. "You'll know next time. I didn't realise you knew about this place." Clara gestured vaguely towards the shop.

Adeline shook her head. "I didn't. Coco led me here."

Clara's eyebrows raised above her sunglasses. "Clever boy."

"Yeah." Adeline felt awkward suddenly, as if she had intruded on Clara's life.

Clara seemed to sense her discomfort and reached out to her. "Come walk with us." She linked her arm through Adeline's. "Were you heading to the park?"

"Yeah," Adeline said again. She glanced back at the shop, as they fell into single file to negotiate the narrow path.

"Witch Way – it's a magical supplies store," Clara said, over her shoulder, as if Adeline had spoken the question in her mind. "Don't worry, they don't sell anything scary. No frog's eyes or dragon blood. At least not in the New Zealand stores."

Adeline could hear the laugh in Clara's voice, and let out a little giggle of her own. "Just non-blood-based magical supplies then?" Honestly, she had no idea what those would be.

Clara smiled. "I was just there for information. I wanted to know if anyone else had felt the energy I've been sensing." They reached the street, and Clara took Adeline's arm again. "Straight on, Lola."

Lola stopped sniffing Coco and snapped back into work-mode at his mistress's command. Adeline transferred Coco's harness to her other hand, to give the dogs a little more space from each other.

"And have they?"

Clara tilted her head, in a non-committal gesture. "Maybe. The owner said a few people have mentioned feeling something, but no one seems to know what it is."

They made their way through Thorndon, to the park. Adeline had always been conscious of the looks she got, when she walked anywhere with Coco, but she quickly learned that had been nothing compared to what it was like with Clara and Lola in tow. People stopped what they were doing, and gaped, fascinated by the two assistance dogs. She guessed they thought she was blind as well, which, in their minds, must make it okay to stare.

She noticed the supermarket manager hovering by the entrance to the building as they approached it. He must be having conniptions, seeing she'd not only come back, but had brought another disabled woman and dog with her. She couldn't help giggling a little at his look of relief when they walked past.

Adeline mulled over what Clara had said. She couldn't deny something strange was happening, but she didn't think she could sense it in the same way Clara could. Yet somehow, some of the witches who frequented the magical supplies shop could. What did that mean? Was it just because she was new to this that she couldn't, or was there something wrong with her? Did all witches just automatically know about that place? Had they all been popping in, buying their witchy supplies for years, while Adeline had been trying to work out why she saw ghosts? What did they even do with magic supplies? The questions circled in her mind but voicing them felt too hard.

Clara stopped, seeming to sense Adeline was spiralling.

"Hey… it's okay, Adeline. We will figure this out."

Adeline nodded. "It's just… I have so many questions, I don't even know where to start."

Clara smiled, kindly. "Just start with one. I'll answer if I can."

"Do I need witchy supplies?" Adeline flushed as soon as the words were out of her mouth, but Clara laughed.

"No. Not every witch does... I think your magic works in a similar way to mine."

This was both comforting and confusing.

"An intention, and an action," Clara continued. She brought her hands together in front of her, as if combining the two pieces. "The action can be anything – reciting a poem, baking some cookies, braiding someone's hair – it doesn't really matter." Clara hesitated, as if thinking over her own words. "Well, it *does* matter. It has to be the *right* action, but that depends on you and what you're trying to do."

Adeline frowned. "But then how do I know what the right action is?"

Clara frowned too, as if she wasn't sure either. "You just... know. You'll understand when you feel it."

Adeline nodded, but she felt disappointed by the answer. She wanted something more solid – a step by step set of instructions and ingredients preferably.

"Besides," Clara added. "The intention is the more important part. It needs to be clear in your mind."

They turned the corner and made their way across the road to the park. They let the dogs off their leads, then they both sat down, taking up the same positions they'd held the day before. Funny how quickly a routine could be established, Adeline thought. She could feel it becoming a familiar thing, dog play dates in the park with Clara stretching out into her future.

"What about the ghosts?" she asked Clara. "And those magic thread things you showed me, what are those?"

Clara frowned again and seemed to be testing out her answer inside her mind before speaking to it. Perhaps she'd never had to try explaining it in layman's terms before. "Ghosts, auras, memories – all of that kind of stuff – it's all just… energy. It's always there, but witches are more sensitive to it, so we pick up on it in ways most people don't."

Again, that raised more questions than it answered. Adeline fell silent, thinking this over. Yesterday, she'd felt excited, as if the world suddenly made more sense. Today, she felt like she was back in kindergarten, desperately trying to figure out even the basics of how things worked. Perhaps it would all get easier with time, but right now, trying to puzzle it all out was giving her a headache.

Clara cleared her throat. "Adeline, I know there are a lot of other things you want to ask me, but can you tell me first, did you find the family tree?"

Adeline sighed. "I didn't. It's complicated, can I show you?"

"Of course."

Clara held out her hand and Adeline clasped it, feeling less self-conscious this time. Across the park, Coco and Lola settled next to each other, sitting side by side as they had the day before. Strangely, it was a relief to see them doing so.

Adeline felt like Coco probably needed a debrief just as much as she did.

She closed her eyes. Letting the memory of the night before flow through her mind. Almost unconsciously, she found herself syncing her breath to Clara's. There was no smoke or colourful coils this time, but she felt a warmth pass between them, as Clara read what had happened from her memory.

Clara drew her hand back. "You're right, the sewing box is important... I just don't know how yet."

That much had been obvious. Coco had been insistent that she needed to stop looking for the family tree and pick up the box. Whatever had thrown it from her hands had been just as insistent that she shouldn't look too closely at it. "I've been too afraid to touch it," she admitted.

Clara nodded. "Sensible. Whatever's trying to stop you is powerful."

Adeline swallowed. She'd known that already, of course. The rumbling in her house had told her all she needed to know about how strong the force she was dealing with really was. There was something different about having someone else voice that aloud though.

"It stopped when I shouted 'drop, cover, hold'. Are those like... magic words, or something?"

Clara let out a little laugh, and Adeline felt her cheeks flush. Clara seemed to realise and smiled kindly at her. "There's no such thing as magic words. It may have given a focus to your magic though – like what I said before, intention and action, saying the phrase being the action in this case."

Adeline shook her head. "But I didn't even know what I was doing!"

Clara shrugged. "A part of you did. And I think the energy that's trapped in your house knew that. I think it realised it couldn't overpower you."

Adeline swallowed. She wasn't sure that was true. She may have floundered her way into stopping it last night, but she had no idea if she'd be able to do it again. "What is it though? Is it the same thing from the supermarket?"

"Probably."

Adeline noticed Clara didn't answer the first part of the question, but she didn't press it. She found a more urgent question spilling from her lips instead. "Why is it coming after me?" She didn't like the petulant tone in her voice, but it was the way she felt. She had barely even known she was a witch – why did some supernatural force have to harass her?

Clara made a noise in her throat. "I don't know. I don't even know if it is coming after *you* specifically. It could just be it found out you were vulnerable without the connection to your family's magic."

Adeline felt a small hint of something she couldn't quite name at that. It wasn't anger exactly, but maybe a sense of abandonment. It wasn't her parents' fault they'd died, of course, but she desperately wished they were here for this. There were so many questions she would never get answers to. Though would they have been any help? She wasn't sure they'd even known magic existed, but she wished they were here for her to at least ask. The loneliness and grief of the past few years bubbled up, mixing with the confusion. She tried to push that aside, knowing none of it was helpful, but it refused to be quashed.

Clara seemed to sense the emotion threatening to overwhelm Adeline, and gently placed a hand on her arm.

"Is it… evil?" Adeline asked. She didn't mean to add drama to the situation, but the last word came out whispered. As soon as she'd voiced the question, she wanted to take it back, unwilling to hear the answer. But Clara shook her head.

"Nothing in nature is evil. Chaotic maybe, but not evil. Someone is using it though – using *you* – and that's what we need to worry about."

"Another witch?"

"Maybe. Though non-magical folk have much more capability for unkindness, and a much greater hunger for power."

Adeline sat back against the bench, the exhaustion and all the information she had just absorbed weighing heavily on her. Sunlight glinted on the surface of the reflection pool in front of them. There was magic in that, she was certain of it. There was magic in all of nature, she could feel it now.

"Sometimes spirits get stronger when they collect energy from other people," Clara said. "It sounds like that's what this one is doing. Collecting a little from each person."

That made sense to Adeline. It was something she'd felt happen in her own life. There were people she always felt tired around, as if they sucked the very life from her, brightening themselves as they did. She'd seen the opposite too, how people could give each other energy freely, seeming to gain some as well in the process. Just like how the auras around passers-by had warmed when she smiled, but doubly so when the person smiled back.

"You said Coco makes my magic stronger. Is it possible Hemi does as well?" She felt embarrassed voicing the question, but she couldn't deny that she'd felt more in control once Hemi arrived, and the ghosts had disappeared as if running from him.

Clara's lips tweaked into a smile, which she tried to suppress. "I think he brings out happiness in you, and happy people are always stronger, witch or not."

Adeline felt a warmth in the way Clara had said that. *He brought out the happiness in her.* She liked the idea that it had been inside her all along, not something he had created for her.

Clara sighed. "You have a strong energetic connection, Adeline. One of the most powerful connections I've ever seen, especially for someone without their family's magic behind them. But you will have to be careful. Your power was dormant for a long time, and it's growing exponentially now." Clara didn't finish the thought, but Adeline sensed the end of it. How much power was too much at once?

"But the energy that I transferred to Hemi – it wasn't

from me, was it? Someone sent it – a ghost." The thought made Adeline's breath catch.

"Yes. From what you've said, I don't think it was Stanley. It probably just found it easier to gain power from another spirit, which is why it started with him." Clara hesitated, thinking. "Adeline, what do you know about the rest of your family?"

Adeline shrugged. "Not much. I don't really have any."

"No cousins? Even if they're removed a few times?"

Adeline shook her head. "Dad was an only child. Mum's family, there was something about a family feud? Several generations back. Mum said her grandparents, or great-grandparents, split off from the rest of the family." Adeline searched her mind for the details but came up blank. She wasn't sure if that was because she'd forgotten them, or if her mum had never known them to pass on in the first place. "I don't know, it was sort of like there was bad blood being passed down through the generations, if that makes sense? People kept falling out or dying early and…" Adeline cut herself off, remembering that's exactly what had happened to her parents too. She swallowed, her mouth feeling very dry suddenly. "Mum used to joke we were cursed." The dry feeling in her throat began to choke Adeline.

Clara reached for her hand and squeezed it firmly once it was in her grasp. "I don't think it's a curse."

Adeline let out a breath. "Good."

"However," Clara continued, and Adeline's stomach sank

at the word. "There are cases where misusing magic can have consequences."

"You think a witch in my family did something wrong?"

"It's very unusual for a magical family to cut members off in the way that you have been. Something very serious must have happened to cause that." Clara let the weight of her words settle over both of them.

Something very serious... What did that mean in the magical sense? A flicker of movement caught Adeline's eye, drawing her away from the conversation.

A transparent figure, with a dark bob cut and fringe, was walking across the park, her hand trailing along the bushes as if she could feel them under her fingertips. Coco and Lola looked up with interest. They both got up, following along behind the ghost, as if she would take them for a walk. Her fingertips left smoky spirals behind her.

"What is it?" Clara asked.

"Katherine Mansfield," Adeline said under her breath. She stood, watching as the author made her way along the top of the bank, heading towards the Lady McKenzie Garden for the Blind.

Clara made a noise in her throat. "I guess the park *is* named after her."

Adeline shook her head. "No, I've never seen her here before. I've never seen any ghosts here before. Coco and Lola are following her."

"Then we should too." Clara took Adeline's arm, and they trailed after the dogs.

Coco glanced back at Adeline to see if she was following and seemed pleased that she was. Adeline trusted him, letting him set the pace. He trotted along, happy that she and Clara had joined the procession, as the author's ghost led them down the zig-zag gravel path. Adeline slowed, seeing Clara's steps were unsure on the rough ground without Lola, not to mention Adeline's own unsteady footing.

"She's going towards the Lady McKenzie Garden," Adeline said. Coco glanced back at her, confirming she was right.

It had originally been a scented garden for the blind. Adeline wasn't sure if that was still the case, but there was a sign in braille she often passed, running her hand over it without knowing the meaning of the words under her fingertips.

Then Adeline noticed another figure coming out of the garden – an older woman Adeline didn't recognise. "I think Lady McKenzie is joining her." She wasn't sure how, but suddenly she was sure that's who the ghost was. The two figures nodded to each other, then each carried on their way, a skip in Katherine Mansfield's step as she walked past. Then slowly, she and Lady McKenzie both faded into nothing.

"They're gone. They just nodded to each other and disappeared."

Clara swallowed. "That's not normal, is it?"

"No, the ghosts don't normally acknowledge each other."

The dogs had stopped, looking confused now the figure leading them had disappeared. Coco padded his way back over to Adeline, nudging her hand.

"Where was she going?"

Adeline patted Coco's head, and Lola trotted over, wanting affection too. "Up to the top bit of the park, where the scented garden is," she told Clara.

"If the dogs were following, we should go check it out. Sometimes they just get confused by supernatural energy, but it could mean something important."

"Okay." Adeline released both dogs, and they took off again towards the Lady McKenzie Garden.

There were tables up there, and a number of people sitting, having lunch. A collective "Aww…" spread around the group, as Coco and Lola entered the paved area, and several people got up to pat them. Adeline watched, horrified, as the smoke she'd seen earlier spread from person to person. A girl stood, and it trailed from her fingertips, just like it had on the ghost's hands.

"Coco, come," Adeline called.

He and Lola rushed back to her, much to the disappointment of the picnickers.

"What's happening?" Clara asked her.

"The smoke, it's here," Adeline whispered.

Clara reached instinctively for Lola's collar. "Don't let it touch the dogs. I don't know what it is, but it shouldn't have access to a familiar's power."

Too late for that, Adeline thought. It was living in her

house. This did seem different from the energy at home, though. More purposeful. She watched as it coiled around one man, and his face paled, just as Hemi's had when the smoke touched him. The man turned abruptly, his steps faltering and unsteady, before he intentionally bumped into someone else and transferred the smoke to them.

Clara shivered, reading the thought in Adeline's mind. "It's possessing them."

Adeline felt sick at the term. It had only been for a few seconds, but she couldn't deny Clara was right. The man hadn't seemed to have control of his actions when the smoke was attached to him.

Adeline glanced over at him. He seemed in control of himself now, but he still looked clammy and pale. He sat back down at one of the tables, hunching over his lunch as if he was going to be ill. Hemi hadn't looked this bad – whatever the smoke was doing to people, it seemed to be getting worse. The smoke was still passing from person to person, each of them reacting in a similar way as it touched them.

"Come on, let's get out of here." Clara refastened Lola's harness and Adeline did the same with Coco's.

They made their way back down to the reflection pool, on the other side of the park. Clara sat beside the water and trailed her hand in it. Adeline did the same, finding comfort in the cool liquid against her skin. She noticed that her friend was shaking. Her own hands were as well.

"What do we do?" she asked Clara.

The older woman just shook her head. "I don't know. This is worse than I thought." Lola nuzzled close to her mistress, and Coco leant against Adeline's legs, offering all the comfort he could.

Adeline felt weak, as if whatever it was they'd encountered was drawing power from her, not just from the people it surrounded.

"You need to rest," Clara said. "You can't fight it if you're exhausted."

"I need to find the family tree," Adeline said, now more fixated on the task than ever.

Clara reached for Adeline's hand, squeezing it when she found it. "One does not preclude the other. You must rest."

Clara was right. If she didn't take care of herself, she would have a seizure, and that would not help anything.

"Okay," she told Clara. "Rest first, then we fight this thing."

CHAPTER SIX

*A*deline didn't go back to work, instead calling her boss to say she was sick then doing as she had promised Clara and going home to lie down. But she couldn't sleep, even with Coco settled protectively beside her. She knew she needed the rest, but her mind was wired, running through what she had seen at the park. More than that, she was mentally searching the house for the box of photos and the family tree. She knew it defeated the purpose of lying down, but she found herself making a plan, knowing exactly where she would look in a step-by-step methodical search.

Eventually, she fell into a restless sleep, ghosts dancing through her dreams. She woke at one point and found the transparent figure of the woman she'd seen earlier with the sewing box, standing over the bed. She stared down at Adeline, and Adeline wasn't sure if she should be afraid. The ghost raised her arm, as if to point, but she was whipped away again, the smoke that made up her outline scattering as if someone had slashed through it with a weapon.

Adeline sunk back down into the depths of a dream.

When she woke again, the ghost was gone, and her head was clearer. Evening sun streamed in through the gap in her curtains, and for a moment, she just enjoyed the beauty of it.

Then she realised her phone was ringing – probably someone from work calling to check on her – and she rolled over onto her stomach to reach for it.

She checked the caller ID, not quite up for dealing with Dana's perkiness, or her boss's worry. But it wasn't either of them, it was Hemi.

She pressed accept call, clearing her throat before answering. "Hello?"

He was out of breath. "It's the weirdest thing," he said, not bothering with a greeting. "No one felt that earthquake, and I mean *no one*."

"Yeah?" Adeline kept her voice neutral.

"Even weirder, I checked Geonet," Hemi continued before she could, "and there was nothing. A couple of tiny shakes earlier in the day, but nothing like what we felt."

Adeline hesitated. She thought about making up a story – going with Dana's idea of it being down to the old house, or their position on the fault line. Instead, she closed her eyes. "I know," she said.

"You know?"

She sighed. "No one at my work felt it either. There's

been... I don't know. There's been some strange things going on." She couldn't quite bring herself to use the words "ghost" or "witch" to him, but she suspected he would hear the implication of something supernatural in her voice.

He was quiet for a moment. "Are you at work?" he asked finally.

Adeline hesitated. "No, I'm at home." She didn't tell him she'd come home sick, but after years of knowing her, and having seen her sent home from school many a time, he could probably fill in the blank.

"Can I come over?" he asked.

Adeline swallowed. She remembered how he had held her after the "earthquake" and how much calmer it had made her feel. Suddenly, all she wanted was to lean her head on his shoulder and have him reassure her it was going to be okay, even if that meant telling him everything.

"Yes, come over," she said.

Hemi greeted Adeline with a hug, exactly as she had hoped, and for a moment, she just wanted to melt into it. But then she remembered what she had to tell him. Her heart broke into a fluttering, panicked pattern and she pulled away from him.

"Do you want something to drink?" she asked, turning towards the kitchen.

"Adeline."

The seriousness in Hemi's voice made her stop, but she couldn't quite make herself face him. Coco plodded his way over to her, gently pressing against her legs as if to herd her back towards Hemi.

When she refused, he turned to Hemi instead, greeting him excitedly, and drawing him over to Adeline. Hemi was a much more agreeable subject, and followed easily, placing his hand on Adeline's shoulder. He stooped his head, trying to meet her eye. She resisted at first, then raised her gaze to his.

There was fear in his eyes, but it was *for* her, not of her.

"What's going on?" he asked.

She swallowed, her mouth incredibly dry suddenly. "I see ghosts," she said. She let out a giggle, realising she'd almost said, "I see dead people" and how inappropriate that would have been. The giggles kept coming, and then she was shaking with them.

Hemi frowned, but his hand remained on her shoulder, not pulling away at least.

"I'm not joking," she said. "I don't know why I'm laughing." And just like that, the giggles disappeared in a puff of air.

She swallowed again, though it made no difference to her sandpaper mouth. She waited, searching Hemi's face for any kind of reaction, but he just kept frowning.

"I know," he said finally. "But what does that have to do with the earthquake?"

Now it was Adeline's turn to frown. "You know?"

Hemi nodded. "You told me years ago. My grandmother saw them too."

Adeline had a sudden memory-flash of sitting in Hemi's treehouse, telling him all of her secrets and him telling all of his. She remembered the sun coming in between the slats of the treehouse roof, making lines across their skin, his eyes closed as he'd listened to everything she'd said.

"You believed me," she said. *No one else ever did*, she nearly added.

"Of course."

He left it at that, but his hand moved gently on her arm, reassuring her. He always seemed to trust in her, in a way she wasn't quite sure she deserved.

"Come," Hemi said, leading her gently to sit with him on the couch. "Tell me."

She told him everything. She had meant to hold back the word "witch" but it came out anyway, though perhaps it sounded more like "witc—" as her voice shut down at the last moment.

She found she couldn't meet his eye when she told him about the energy transferring from her to him, but he reached out, his palm pressing gently against her skin again, as if to absolve her of the guilt she'd built up around it.

His silence continued as she explained about the sewing box, and the power that had rattled the house, throwing it from her hands. Coco wandered over, laying down between them, his warm body pressing against their legs, as if to reassure both of them. Hemi patted him, but it seemed to be unconsciously; his eyes never strayed from Adeline's face.

Her voice began to die in her throat. She wondered if he thought her crazy, but she made herself continue. She had gotten this far, she might as well finish. She told him about the smoke she and Clara had seen at the park, the way it had seemed to possess people, forcing them to bump into each other so it could transfer on. Even as she spoke, a part of her wondered if telling him all this was a form of self-sabotage – she'd had a habit of destroying relationships before they got started in the past.

"And then Clara sent me home, to rest. I saw the ghost again, but she was whipped away before she said anything. She was trying to point at something, but... I don't know, it could have been a dream," she finished lamely.

Hemi took a breath, and she realised she needed to do the same, having been speaking in a rush for far too long. His eyelids were fluttering, and she could almost see the thoughts playing behind them. She bit the tip of her tongue, stopping herself from filling the silence with more prattling. He would need time to process, she understood that, but she desperately needed him to say at least *something*. Otherwise, all she could assume was that he thought her insane.

He stood suddenly, displacing Coco. Adeline's stomach dropped, and she fought hard to keep her face neutral. Of course he was leaving; who wouldn't after all this? But then he reached down to help her up.

"Which way did she point?" he asked.

"I don't know." Adeline's knee protested at the idea of straightening after sitting for so long, and she leaned on Hemi's hand heavier than she would have liked. "She disappeared before she really could. It was like someone attacked her."

He made a noise in his throat, thinking. "Do you think we could guess? If you stood where she was standing?"

Adeline shrugged. "Maybe? Worth a try." Her heart was racing, but she couldn't tell whether it was in excitement or anxiety. He was still here. He'd heard everything she had to say, and he was still here. Not only that, he was here and helping her.

"Come on." He took her hand again, leading the way.

She stumbled, her leg resisting the movement, and the idea of climbing the stairs. Hemi stopped abruptly, turning back to her. She braced herself, ready for him to change his mind or ask: "You don't really mean *ghosts* do you?" Instead, he pulled her into a fierce hug. She squeezed him back, feeling all the comfort she had wanted earlier.

He drew away, but kept his hand on her arm, moving it gently, reassuring her. "You can trust me, you know?" he said.

Adeline's breath came out in a rush. There was so much more behind that, she could feel it. He was thanking her for telling him, promising to believe her – or at least to always try to believe her – no matter how deep into the supernatural her life went. More than that, he was saying he wanted to be a part of it. She could feel the years of their shared history wrapping around her, making her feel safer than she had in a long time.

"I know."

Adeline stood with her arm raised, approximating where the ghost had been. She traced the path the spirit's hand had made, before disappearing into nothing. "Like this, I think."

Hemi stepped out into the corridor, following the path. "You're pointing at the wall," he said eventually.

Adeline dropped her hand, deflated. "Maybe I'm remembering it wrong? I don't know."

Hemi leant against the doorframe. "I can still help you look."

She could hear the dubious note in his voice. One quick glance around her place would have told him all he needed to know about her tidiness level. At least there were no bras on the doorknob this time.

She nodded regardless, stepping towards him. "If you don't mind, that would be great. I was going to check Mum and Dad's room next."

She still called it that, though it had been years since her parents had occupied it, and she'd had many a guest stay in the time since. It would still always be their room, no matter how many years passed or personal items she gave away.

They sat on the floor, sorting through her parents' papers and looking for the missing photographs and family tree. It helped to have him there. By herself, she would have easily got distracted by all the memories and emotions that came up.

"I was sorry to hear about what happened to your family, Adey."

Adeline nodded. It had been years since the car accident, and she didn't know how to respond when people expressed sympathy. There was always a battle inside her when the subject came up. Partly to keep her emotions in check, but also the strange guilt that came with worrying she wasn't sad *enough*. For her, their deaths were a long time ago. She *was* sad, but she was also okay, and sometimes she wondered if she shouldn't be – if people thought her callous for not drowning in it every time they mentioned it.

Hemi was chewing on the inside of his lip, watching her. "I wanted to get in touch, when I found out, but it had been two years by then, and it just felt…" He shrugged, unable to find the words. "I should have been there for you when it happened."

Adeline shook her head. "It's okay. You couldn't have known."

"Still. I wish I'd been here." He squeezed her hand, and she felt like he was pouring their years of history into the gesture. "They were like a second set of parents to me growing up."

"They loved you too," she told him. Her parents had cared about all her friends, but she knew Hemi had held a special place in their home. "You were always welcome here. Always *are*."

Coco made a contented little grunting noise, in the back of his throat, as if he agreed with her words.

It was weird. She and Hemi had been so close when they were teenagers. She had stayed in touch with plenty of people from her school days... but not him. He'd gone travelling straight away, and at first, she'd tried to stay up to message him or call him at least once a week, but the time differences got harder and harder. Once she started university, it was basically impossible. Besides, talking to him when he was so far away had made her sad. Missing him had been like a physical pain, and instead of easing when they finally did manage to chat, the gaps she found in her knowledge about his life made that wound a little deeper. It hadn't been a conscious decision from either of them to stop talking, the messages had just slowly petered out, until one day she realised she hadn't spoken to him in years.

Hemi reached out, squeezing her hand as if sensing all that was going through her head. He was here now. She gripped his hand a little tighter, reassuring herself of that. His eyes traced over her face as if looking for something there. He smiled, and a little twist of hope started up in her stomach, thinking perhaps he'd found it.

Then suddenly she felt cold. Something shifted, almost like everything had turned monochrome. She pulled away from Hemi, scanning the room.

"What is it?" he asked.

Adeline pressed a finger to Hemi's lips, shushing him. She looked to Coco. His head was raised, eyes and ears alert, but he wasn't growling. She took that as a good sign.

"I think a ghost might be here," she whispered.

A figure appeared, gradually materialising into the woman she'd seen earlier. The ghost touched a finger to her own lips, calling for stillness. Adeline held her breath, not wanting to cause even the smallest disruption. She felt Hemi instinctively do the same.

The ghost raised her arm slowly, pointing. Adeline followed the line, her eyes landing on a spot on the wall, exactly where Hemi had told her she'd pointed before.

"I don't understand," Adeline said aloud.

The ghost raised her finger to her lips again. Her eyes widened, and she glanced nervously over her shoulder. Adeline bit her tongue, holding back her questions. Finally, the ghost raised her arm again. She jiggled her hand as if to insist.

"What's she doing?" Hemi asked.

Adeline shook her head. "Pointing at the wall again."

The ghost stiffened, tension written across her face.

Adeline froze for a moment, then stood, slowly. "I think she's afraid of someone hearing us," she said under her breath to Hemi.

He nodded and followed her lead, easing himself up from the ground gently. They made their way over to the wall, stepping lightly to avoid creaks in the floorboards. The ghost followed them. Adeline shivered, but the smoky outline of her ancestor blurred and reformed around them, fitting herself to the available space rather than passing through.

"Here?" Hemi whispered, running his hand over the wall.

Adeline nodded, frustration making the movement jerky. Hemi gave a sharp inhale, as his hand caught on something. He pulled away from the wall, and she instinctively took his hand in hers, as if she could heal the scratch just with her touch. His fingers curled down over hers, and he stepped towards her, almost as if they were drawing each other in.

"I didn't see the picture hook," he said.

Adeline touched the nail, carefully. It was the same colour as the wallpaper, blending in to the point of disappearing, but the bent edge was sharp.

"There used to be a picture here. It was a flower, or a garden, something like…" As she spoke, an image of the painting came clear in her mind. It was of a little girl, holding a watering can. Her mum had always said it reminded her of Adeline. The little girl's mother hovered in the background, standing in front of a green, wooden shed.

"The shed!" Adeline's voice rose in excitement.

Hemi rushed to shush her, but it was too late. A look of horror crossed the ghost's face. "Go now!" she mouthed, then her head jerked around, and she flinched, dodging an invisible blow. She took one step, breaking into a run, and then she was gone.

A rumbling sound crept up around them. Adeline grabbed Hemi's hand. "Come on."

They raced down the stairs as the walls around them began to shake. A whine rose in Coco's throat.

"Where are we going?" Hemi yelled over the noise.

"The shed. I put some boxes out there when I was trying to tidy up." She didn't need to add that she hadn't got very far in her efforts. They made it to the kitchen, and Adeline shrieked as a plate flew off the bench towards them. Hemi grabbed her, and together they crouched over Coco, covering their heads.

"We need to get outside. It will stop once we're outside." Adeline wasn't sure how she knew that, but she was learning to trust her instincts. She felt Hemi hesitate. All their lives, they'd been taught not to run outside during a quake. But this was no ordinary seismic event.

She circled his wrist with her hand, pouring all the reassurance she could into him through her palm.

He took a breath. "Okay, let's go."

Coco took off ahead of them, understanding their intentions almost before they did. Adeline scrabbled with the key in the back door, opening it and shooting out into the back yard. The earth's shaking stopped instantly, but the tremors inside her didn't. She pressed trembling hands to her face, and Hemi pulled her into a hug.

"You okay?" he asked.

She nodded. "You?"

"Yeah, I'm fine." His eyes were wide, and he was shaking just as much as she was. She could see there was an exhilaration behind it, though. He always had been a bit of an adrenaline junky. That hadn't been a part of his life she thought she would ever share, but she hadn't counted on her supernatural ancestry finding them.

Coco trotted over to the shed, his tail wagging, the earlier fear evidently forgotten. Adeline reluctantly pulled away from Hemi, moving over to the shed. It was padlocked, but the key was on the same ring as the back door one.

"Is stuff going to start flying in here too?" he asked.

Adeline shook her head. "I don't know." They looked around, but nothing moved. Everything was still and peaceful. "Maybe they can't leave the house? That could be why she pointed to the missing picture?"

Hemi shrugged. "Maybe."

It was a creative solution if that was the case, though Adeline wondered why the ghost hadn't just talked to her. She fitted the key into the lock, but it was stiff, refusing to turn.

"I thought they always said ghosts haunted people not places," Hemi added. "Like, they're not just hanging out in the places they died, are they?"

Adeline shook her head. "No, I don't think so. I see Katherine Mansfield quite often, and she died in France."

Adeline also didn't think they haunted people, or she was sure she would have seen her parents at least once. "Most of the ghosts I see, I don't think they're haunting anything. They're just... energy left behind."

"Like memories?"

"Yeah, maybe." Memories of what though? Or perhaps the better question would be, from whom? Perhaps they were just moments that had made the people happy; moments they wanted to revisit. Adeline liked that idea.

She jiggled the lock, but it wouldn't budge. She could see Hemi was biting his tongue, trying not to offer to take over, and that just made her more determined to open it herself.

She gave the key one last fierce twist, and the lock finally sprung apart. Hemi creaked the door open, then took out his phone to light the inside.

Adeline stepped closer to him, and she felt Coco press against her leg on the other side, reassuring her. Though she kept good care of the garden, she never used the shed. It had always scared her as a child, and so it had become a place to store stuff rather than a functional building.

Strangely, though, as soon as she was inside, she didn't feel that fear anymore. A warmth filled her, and she felt herself drawn to a particular box.

"This one," she said, certainty filling her voice.

"Are you sure?" Hemi moved the torch on his phone around, revealing five other identical white plastic tubs.

"Yes, I'm sure."

Coco made a soft sound, almost like he was saying the

word "woof". She took it as his approval. He turned, trotting back towards the house. He paused on the back doorstep, looking over his shoulder as if to check they were coming.

Hemi shrugged, clearly confused, but trusting them. He and Adeline hefted the box up between them, carrying it back to the house.

They found the family tree and old photos straight away, though it ended up being a bit of an anticlimax. Somehow, Adeline had thought she would find the box, and everything would immediately become clear. Instead, they were sitting on the floor again, staring at a bunch of sepia-toned faces and crinkled paper.

Hemi traced his finger in the air above the lines of her ancestors on the family tree. "You reckon she's your great-grandmother?" he asked.

"Great-great, I think? I don't know. Maybe I can work it out from the clothing style."

"Charles Anderson married to Millicent Dove-some-thing," Hemi read from the page. "The end of her name is missing, but they would be your great-great-grandparents on your mother's side. One set of them anyway."

Adeline read over his shoulder, following the lines of scrawly handwriting where he indicated. The page had torn and been taped back together, a small corner missing, truncating Millicent's surname. It sounded familiar though.

"Dover, I think. It was written on the back of one of the photos." She flipped over some of the pictures she'd laid out, looking for Millicent's.

"Here's one of Charles," Hemi said, picking up a photo of a man with thick glasses and facial hair.

"Oh, it's severe moustache-man!" It wasn't the same photo as the one on the wall in the corridor, but it was definitely the same man. "There's a photo of him upstairs," she told Hemi. "His eyes follow you when you walk past. It always used to creep me out as a kid."

He chuckled at her explanation, and she moved the photo back and forth, noting that this one did the same. Still creepy, even as an adult. Hemi placed it on the tree, next to the name.

"Here's Millicent," he said, picking up another photo and holding it out to Adeline.

She studied it. The ghost's face had been thinner, her cheekbones more pronounced and her eyes closer together. "That's not who I saw. She was younger."

"Not an older version of her?" Hemi asked.

Adeline shook her head. "I don't think so. Besides, if she's a ghost, presumably she didn't get any older?" The thought sobered both of them. The spirit's fear worried Adeline. What had she risked to give Adeline that message? What was there that could scare a ghost? She shivered at the idea.

Hemi put down the photo he was holding, and sat back, obviously feeling just as defeated as she was. "Maybe we should stop for tonight. I don't think we're going to figure anything else out now."

Adeline nodded, a yawn bubbling up inside her at the suggestion. Coco was already asleep, using her foot as a pillow. "True. I'll call Clara tomorrow. She might have some ideas."

"Good thinking." Hemi's lips parted, but then he just took a breath and let it out again without speaking.

Adeline nudged his shoulder with hers. "Spit it out."

"What?"

She nudged him again. "Come on, you think I don't know your 'I don't know if I should say that' face?" She grinned and was delighted to see he blushed a little.

"Yeah, true." He laughed, then shook his head. "I was just going to ask if I could stay… on the couch, of course," he added quickly. "I just don't want you to be alone if…" he waved his hand, gesturing to the room around them, "whatever *that* was happens again."

Adeline hesitated, feeling a twist of anxiety in her stomach. Rather than reassuring her, him wanting to stay just reminded her there was a reason to be afraid. She almost said no, wanting to try fool herself into believing everything was fine. But the memories of the "earthquakes" flooded through her and she found herself wanting to cling to him.

She took a slow breath, letting the anxiety inside her unknot itself as she did. "Yes, I'd like that. You can stay. But you don't need to sleep on the couch, this house has far too many spare rooms for that."

He grinned. "No comments about not rescuing you?"

Adeline couldn't help but laugh, but it was short-lived, the fear creeping back in a little. She wasn't sure Hemi could protect her from *whatever that was* but her heart squeezed a little at the thought that he wanted to try.

She reached for his hand. "I think we'll be rescuing each other," she said.

CHAPTER SEVEN

*A*deline woke suddenly in the night. She could hear Hemi snoring from the spare room, a little rumble on every second exhale, but that wasn't what had disturbed her. She'd been dreaming about the ghost. She'd heard her singing in the other room, a song Adeline's mum used to hum whenever she was painting or sewing... *Sewing*. The ghost was trying to lead her back to the sewing box.

Adeline groaned, then closed her eyes and rolled on to her side. Rather than irritating her, the sound of Hemi's snoring was reassuring. She'd forgotten how comforting it was to have someone else in the house overnight.

She knew her fear of picking up the box was irrational. The earthquakes had come back, even when she left it lying on the floor, so there was no reason to keep avoiding it. A part of her wondered if it was less about being afraid, and more about the frustration she felt not knowing what it all meant. What on earth was she supposed to do with a sewing box? Perhaps the ghost just wanted her to help mend a button.

Adeline smiled at her own joke, but something tugged at her memory. *Mending...* She opened her eyes. How could she have not thought of it earlier? She got out of bed, stepping lightly to avoid the creaky floorboards waking Hemi. Coco peered up at her from his position beside the bed. She pressed her finger to her lips, and he seemed to understand, lowering his head to his blanket.

Adeline padded out into the corridor, shivering in the cold air. She stared up at the trapdoor in the ceiling. The night's shadows seemed to make little arrows, all of them pointing towards the attic, coaxing her to go up there.

"Are you okay, Adey?"

Adeline jumped at the sound of Hemi's voice. He appeared in the spare room doorway, Coco beside him, wagging his tail. Adeline frowned at the dog. He'd probably trotted off to the other room as soon as she was gone, waking Hemi up and giving her away.

Adeline glanced down at Hemi's boxer shorts. "Are you... Are those Ninja Turtles?"

Hemi gave a sleepy grin and struck a pose. "They go with your bra."

Adeline shook her head. "Is it creepy or cute that we own matching underwear?"

Hemi just laughed in response. Adeline loved the sound of his laugh, but she couldn't help her eyes drifting back towards the trapdoor. Was she imagining it, or were the arrow-like shadows stretching out longer, as if to highlight that's where her attention should be?

Hemi's laughter petered out, his face slipping towards a frown. "What is it, Adey? What's going on?"

Adeline hesitated. A part of her wanted him to go back to bed so she could investigate alone. At the same time, he had promised to trust her and that meant she had to at least try to trust him in return. "There was a quilt..." she said finally. "Just before all this started, I ripped it in the attic."

"Yeah?" Hemi rubbed his eyes.

"I fell, and there was this cloud of dust. It almost looked like it was going to turn into a ghost, but then it just settled over me." Adeline froze as she remembered what had happened next. "When Stanley grabbed me in the supermarket, he dislodged the dust. It was swirling and mixing with the smoke."

Hemi crossed his arms, goosebumps appearing on his bare skin above the boxers. She realised she was staring at his chest and looked away, blushing.

"So... you think the ghost was in the quilt?"

She could hear the dubious note in his voice, and the heat in her cheeks intensified. "I'm sorry, this is silly. Go back to bed."

He glanced towards his room, clearly tempted. "Nah, I'm up now," he said. "What are you thinking?"

"I don't know. Perhaps it's nothing, but it's strange timing isn't it?"

He shrugged, and she could see he was holding back a yawn. "It's worth checking out, I guess."

She smiled, relieved he wasn't irritated with her. "I figured that might be what the sewing box is about," she said as she grabbed the metal pole which hung on the bathroom doorframe and used the plastic key on the end of it to unlatch the trapdoor. "Maybe it's been about mending the quilt the whole time?"

"Makes as much sense as anything else." He helped her pull down the ladder, then climbed up the first few rungs before she had a chance to object.

"Where is it?" he called, once he was inside the roof.

"In a box on the left-hand side. It should be obvious; I didn't put it away properly."

She heard him stumble, then some muffled rustling. She really shouldn't have let him go up there without a torch. After a moment, he reappeared at the head of the ladder with the quilt in his arms. "Can I throw it down to you?"

"Sure."

He tossed the quilt to her, then climbed down himself. Adeline coughed as dust caught in her throat, but nothing else happened.

"What do you think? We mend the tear, and see if that changes anything?" Hemi ran his hand over his hair. It stuck up in spiky, black clumps, and his eyes were red-rimmed, itching to go back to sleep.

"Yeah… maybe." Now the quilt was in her arms, Adeline felt less certain that it was significant. There was no rumbling in the walls, nor any objects flying towards them. The force in the house had desperately tried to stop them from reaching the sewing box and the family tree, while Coco and the ghost tried equally hard to lead them to them. Coco gave the quilt a cursory sniff, but nothing else supernatural seemed remotely interested.

Hemi touched her shoulder gently, then took the quilt from her to carry it downstairs. "It's worth a shot, eh?"

Adeline was too nervous to pick up the sewing box again, instead grabbing a needle and thread from her own sewing kit. She let Coco sniff them and he seemed to approve. She looked up and found Hemi watching this exchange, a bemused smile on his face.

"No shaking, at least," she said.

"True."

They spread the quilt out over them on the couch, and Adeline uncoiled a length of thread.

"Got a second needle?" Hemi asked, but Adeline hesitated, closing her hand over the thread.

"You don't have to stay up. You can go back to sleep, if you want."

Hemi raised his eyebrows. "Really, Adey?" His leg shifted under the quilt, and she felt the warmth of his knee against hers. "You think I'm going to leave you here doing... witchy tapestry by yourself when it might start another earthquake?"

She flushed, embarrassed by him putting it like that. "It's not a tapestry."

Hemi chuckled. "Fine, witchy-powered quilting, whatever. I'm still not leaving." He leant back against the couch and watched her with half-closed eyes.

Adeline bit her tongue, swallowing another comment about him trying to rescue her. Maybe, she conceded, ghosts infiltrating her house was a valid enough reason to need a bit of help. Emphasis on the help, though – she still didn't need rescuing.

Coco sighed, having been relegated to his own bed, now that the couch was covered by the quilt. Adeline wet the end of the thread on her lips, looping it through the eye of the needle and securing it with a knot at the end. She wasn't sure if there were any "witchy powers" in the routine, but she found the methodical steps to sewing soothing. It was something she'd learnt from her mother, and it felt like an act of remembrance to do it now.

Hemi smoothed out the fabric as she mended the tear. "Look, it's a tree," he said.

Adeline glanced down, taking in the whole quilt for the first time. "Oh yeah."

Before, she'd only been looking at the trails of tiny stitches and the individually floral-patterned fabrics. She'd missed the shape they made when combined. The pink and brown patches made up the trunk and branches of the tree, the green diamonds becoming the leaves.

"I wonder if she made it," she said.

"The ghost?"

Adeline nodded. "Yeah, it feels like it could have been hers."

Hemi shrugged. "Could be."

He hadn't moved his leg from beside hers, and she liked feeling the warmth coming from him being close. Coco propped his head on her foot, and it was like they were both leaning in to support her. She stitched for a few minutes, the silence companionable.

When she glanced at Hemi, she found him smiling at her. "Tell me a story," she said, using a childlike voice.

Hemi blinked then took a big breath. "There once was a man from—"

"No!" Adeline kicked his leg, giggling. "Tell me a story from when you were away."

Hemi went quiet again. "I think I told you them all the other night."

"Why'd you come back?"

Hemi's smile faltered, and he looked away. "I don't know. I missed home."

Adeline frowned. There was clearly more to it. She kept stitching, giving him the opportunity to tell her if he wanted, but not forcing the issue.

"I was dating this girl," he said finally. He glanced at her, and Adeline felt a strange little flip in her stomach.

"She wanted to get serious – marriage and stuff – and I liked her and all, but she never felt like... home."

Adeline could understand that. She'd had partners over the years, and she'd felt something similar. She'd never expected any one person to be her everything, but she also couldn't cope with them feeling like an intruder in her life.

Hemi glanced down at the fabric in her hands. "Looks like you've nearly finished."

Adeline nodded. She looped the thread underneath itself a few times, then cut the needle free.

"Do you feel any different?" Hemi asked, after a moment's silence.

Adeline found herself holding her breath, waiting. "No," she said finally. "I don't think that fixed anything."

"Except the quilt." A cheeky smile played at the corners of Hemi's lips.

"Except the quilt," Adeline agreed. She couldn't help feeling a little deflated. For a second, she had been sure this was the answer to everything, but all it had done was keep them up half the night. So much for her promise to Clara that she would rest.

"Hey, it was worth a shot, right?"

"Right."

His gaze traced over her face. "You look tired."

Adeline rolled her eyes. "Thanks."

He chuckled. "I just meant we should try get some sleep."

Adeline nodded, the deflated feeling increasing. "Thank you for staying up with me."

"Of course."

The silence hung for a moment. She knew she should stand up, go back to bed so they could both rest. But instead, she was staring into his eyes, and he was staring back, the little smile still playing on his lips.

"I'm glad you came home," she said.

"Me too."

Hemi feels like my *home.* The thought came into her mind unbidden. She reached for him, wanting to grab his hand again. At the same time, he went to brush the hair from her face. They laughed as their arms collided, ending up fumbling as their fingers intertwined.

How many times had she reached for him over the past few days? How many times had he touched her arm, or pulled her into a hug?

"Hemi…" she said, but she didn't get any further than that.

Instead, his hand moved to her cheek, no collision this time, just the softness of his fingers brushing over her skin. Then his mouth found hers, and they kissed.

His lips were dry, but they had the faintest taste of honey. She kissed him back, feeling warmth spread up her body as his arms wrapped around her. His hand pressed against the small of her back, in the gap between the shorts and top of her pyjamas. She felt like every nerve ending was waking up, reaching out to draw him closer.

He pulled her towards him, and her lips fought between trying to smile and kiss at the same time. It was strange how

HELEN VIVIENNE FLETCHER

right this felt – no awkwardness, no insecurity. Just her and him, best friends always.

He drew back, leaving his forehead resting against hers. "Hi," he said softly.

She grinned. "Hi."

His hand moved to her neck, tracing a pattern on her collarbone with his thumb. "I've been wanting to do that for three days."

Adeline laughed. "Try since we were 15." She blushed, regretting the words as soon as they were out of her mouth.

Hemi's eyes widened, and for a moment she thought she'd scared him off, but then his face broke back into a delighted smile. "Why didn't you tell me?"

Adeline just shook her head, embarrassed.

He pulled her close, chuckling as he kissed her again. She found her hands moving to his hair, running her fingers through it like she'd wanted to for days – years.

Finally, they broke apart, sheepishly smiling at each other.

Hemi's gaze flicked to her lips again. "I guess I should let you get some sleep."

Adeline made a face, laughing. "You think I'm going to be able to sleep, now?" Even as she said it, she could feel a yawn building in her throat.

"Come here." He lay back on the couch, pulling her on to his chest. The couch was too small for both of them, really, but somehow it was amazingly comfortable. She liked the feeling of being tucked up like that – there was something

100

so secure about lying wrapped in his arms. She just hoped he wasn't suffocating, squished underneath her.

He stroked her forehead, kissing her gently, and some of the tension from the last few days eased, slipping away with each brush of his hand across her skin.

"You're putting a spell on me," she whispered. A part of her wondered if it was true.

"Yes, I am," he whispered back. "Go to sleep, Adey."

And like magic, she felt her eyes closing.

CHAPTER EIGHT

*A*deline waited for Clara in the park the next day, but her thoughts kept straying back to Hemi every few seconds.

No, focus, she told herself. If Clara was right, and something bad was coming, she couldn't let herself get caught up, no matter how delicious it had been waking up with him lying next to her.

She'd brought the photos of Millicent and Charles with her in the hopes that Clara might be able to glean something from them. It seemed unlikely, especially as Adeline was certain Millicent wasn't the ghost she'd seen, but at this point, it was her only idea.

Coco was playing with a golden retriever, the two of them rolling around in the grass. Adeline was happy to see that. As thankful as she was for the help he gave her – both as an assistance dog and now as a familiar – it was important he still had time to just be a dog.

Adeline nodded to the other owner – a frail older woman who seemed unsteady on her feet. Not exactly ideal with two large, excited dogs running around. On another day, Adeline might have struck up a conversation, but right now her mind was too busy. Instead, she smiled awkwardly each time she met the woman's eye, and hovered, ready to intervene if Coco got too close. Most of the time they both kept their focus on the dogs.

A springer spaniel suddenly appeared, startling Adeline. He raced in a loop around Coco and his friend, before doubling back and jumping up on her.

"Off! Down, no!" she called out, but the spaniel ignored her, too excited to listen to commands.

Coco raised his head, watching cautiously as she interacted with the other dog. Adeline glanced around for the spaniel's owner but couldn't see anyone.

The spaniel rushed over to the older lady, jumping up on her and nearly bowling her over.

"Off!" Adeline said firmly, taking hold of the spaniel's collar. "Are you okay?" she asked the woman.

The woman nodded. "I'm okay, just not used to all this excitement." She raised her hand, curling her fingers down into her palm. "Sit!"

The spaniel sat, much more willing to pay attention now he was captured. His tail still wagged in the grass, though, and he watched the woman attentively.

Adeline laughed as she realised Coco and the golden

retriever were sitting too, eyes focused on Adeline as they waited for either a treat or another command.

"Oh, I'm so sorry!" A man rushed across the park towards them. "He got out the gate, and he's much too fast for me."

The spaniel stood up, excited to see his human, but Adeline kept hold of his collar just in case.

"Did you take yourself on an adventure?" Adeline asked the spaniel. He wagged his tail at her, not showing the least bit of remorse.

"He keeps getting out. I don't know what I'm going to do with him." The man reached out to clip the spaniel back on to his lead.

Coco let out a growl. Adeline looked up, alarmed. She saw the smoke around the man's arm, just before he touched the golden retriever's owner.

"No!" She pulled the lady back. They both looked startled, but Adeline didn't care. Coco raced over, putting himself between Adeline and the danger.

The man frowned. His face was pale and held the same sheen of sweat the other victims of the smoke had. As Adeline watched, she noticed his hands were shaking, and his breathing was laboured. The smoke really was a parasite, leeching off people.

Adeline glanced at the older woman, then back at the man. If the smoke could have that effect on a young, healthy person, what would it do to someone as frail as this lady?

For a moment, nothing happened. The woman laughed

nervously, and the man blinked, seeming to waver between confusion and annoyance at her strange behaviour. Then the smoke reappeared around him. It took the shape of a person, hovering just above his skin. Adeline saw the hint of eyes, the outline of lips, and above them, a suggestion of facial hair. There was something familiar about it.

"Who are you?" she asked.

Without meaning to, she stepped forward, almost as if she was being drawn to him. The smoke jumped the gap. It coiled its way up her arm, slithering over her skin.

"No!" She stepped back, slapping at it, but the ghostly wisps were stuck firmly to her. "Oh no, no, no, no!" She could feel it already, sucking the energy, the very life out of her.

The man's confusion gave way to anger. "Just give me my dog, lady!"

Adeline realised she was still holding the spaniel's collar and released it, letting the dog run back to his owner. Coco whined, but Adeline backed away, remembering Clara's words about not letting the smoke touch the familiars.

"Are you alright, love?" The woman reached out to her, and Adeline dodged away, not wanting to pass the smoke on after all this.

It was creeping over her face now, clouding her vision. The woman's eyes widened, seeming to sense some of the supernatural energy. She stepped back, suddenly afraid.

Adeline opened her mouth, but the smoke coiled over her lips, tiny particles moving as one. Each was unique, different patterns and colours coming together, little bits of energy, all controlled by this writhing, moving swirl.

Was each one of these from a different person?

As soon as that thought entered her mind, she felt as if she was being pulled apart, stretching out like the tiny strands of a rope being frayed. She could feel all of them. Every single spirit in the city, alive and dead, all of them piled one on top of the other. The grey spirals of their energy all reached for her at once, bursting through her and coming out into this world. She threw her hands over her ears as her head exploded with the noise.

She saw Coco trying to get to her, giving his seizure alert, but it was too late. She felt herself start to fall, saw the man and woman diving forward to catch her. Then everything imploded into light.

"Adeline… Adeline!"

She sucked in a breath and opened her eyes, at the sound of Clara's voice. Coco, Lola and Clara were all gathered around her, Clara's hands protecting her head from hitting back against the gravel path beneath her.

She swallowed, tasting blood in her mouth. Her eyes were unfocused, but her mind felt much clearer than it normally did after a seizure. She had a feeling Clara and Lola had something to do with that.

"Just rest." Clara stroked the hair back from Adeline's

face, and Adeline found herself crying. Clara's touch was so gentle, so soothing. Adeline thought of her mother's hands, the way they had held her and comforted her after her seizures, and at so many other times.

"Magic can be hard on both the mind and the body at first," Clara said softly. "I suspect yours has been taking a heavy toll with no one to help you through it."

Clara's hands slowed their movement, coming to rest gently on Adeline's forehead, and Coco and Lola both lay down, one on each side of Adeline, supporting her.

She shivered, remembering the smoke, and tried to pull away from the dogs. "The smoke..." she said, her mouth feeling thick. "It shouldn't touch—"

"It's gone. There was a crowd around you by the time I got here, I felt it moving away."

Adeline closed her eyes, sinking down into the darkness behind her lids. She could still feel it – all the energy behind the smoke. It prickled in her veins, like little electric shocks, as if to remind her how powerful it was.

"I tried to stop it – to save that woman," she told Clara, "but all I did was scare her."

Clara didn't answer. Instead, she raised her face to the sky, as if to warm it in the sun. She sat like that for a moment, and Adeline found her own skin warming and her heart rate slowing. She felt as if Clara was wrapping her in a bubble of love and kindness. She felt safe and relaxed for the first time in a long while. No, not the first time. She had felt that when Hemi wrapped his arms around her too.

"People have always been afraid of witches, it's not your fault Adeline," Clara said finally.

Adeline nodded. It wasn't something she had experienced first-hand before, having only just learned she was a witch, but she had seen the reactions to her stories of seeing ghosts as a child. There was a reason she had learned to stay silent.

"You were brave. You tried very hard to fight against that spirit, but it's been collecting energy for days now. It used your own power against you."

She had no idea how to fight this, no idea how to even understand it. It was so strong, connecting to so many people and other ghosts. What could she do when she was all alone against it?

"You're not alone," Clara said, as if Adeline had spoken aloud. She smoothed the side of Adeline's face. "I believe you and I are connected... even family maybe. I'm still not sure how, but I can feel it. I think you can too."

Adeline hesitated. *I don't have any family,* came the automatic thought. She felt her walls going up, bringing her back to the loneliness of her empty house.

Coco nudged her hand, pushing it up and licking it. Adeline looked up at Clara. She did feel safe when they were together. Though the woman couldn't be more than fifteen years older than her, she'd felt like she was with her mother – with someone she was connected to. "Yes, I do," she said finally. "I feel it." The words made an ache start up in her chest. She wanted to cry with a mix of joy and pain.

Clara squeezed Adeline's shoulder, as if to reassure her she understood the rush of emotions Adeline was going through.

Clara opened her mouth, but then shut it without saying anything. "The thing is, there are burdens that come with that," she said eventually. "In my family, our powers have always been strong. Too strong for us to handle at times, and enough to draw the attention of others."

Adeline nodded, tears forming again. The way the golden retriever's owner had looked at her, the fear in her eyes when she'd seemed to sense the energy around Adeline. She saw her as different. She saw her as a threat.

"That fear I mentioned... people have done terrible things because of it. It's a fear that comes from jealousy. They either want to steal our strength or destroy it."

Adeline's breath caught in her throat. This wasn't where she'd thought the conversation was going. "What sort of things?"

Clara sighed. "That is a complicated story."

When was it not? Adeline thought. It felt like a long time since anything had been simple in her life.

"The witches in my family – some of us don't see so well from our eyes," Clara touched her sunglasses. "But the vision from our other senses is strong. It's not just our sight, though. Our minds and bodies often don't work in the expected ways."

Clara fell quiet, and it took Adeline a moment to realise what she was trying to say.

"You mean like my epilepsy."

Clara inclined her head. "Yes, it's one of the illnesses that run in my family."

Adeline had heard all sorts of old wives' tales about seizures over the years, most of them highly offensive. Demons, evil possession, she had heard it all. A part of her wanted to reject what Clara was saying – that witches and epilepsy ran together – for that reason alone. But that didn't seem to be what Clara meant, and she already knew there was nothing evil about being a witch.

Suddenly, another thought occurred to her. "Wait, are you saying all witches are disabled?" Was that why both their assistance dogs were also familiars?

"Not all witches, no, and not all disabled people are witches either. But the ones in my family often are, have always been as far back as any record we can find." Clara paused and when she spoke again, there was a catch in her voice. "It's no coincidence that people have constructed the world in a way that's difficult for disabled people. They believed it would keep our power in check."

Adeline blinked, trying to process that. She'd heard people say things like that before – that it wasn't the disability which made life hard, but the way the world *treated* disabilities which caused the problems.

"Your connection to magic… it's a very powerful thing, and like I said, non-magical folk fear power. They've made the world difficult for blind people, for wheelchair users, for all of us, in the hopes of containing us."

"But how? That would take a... I don't know, a global conspiracy or something." Adeline felt silly using the word "conspiracy" but at the same time, it seemed to be the only one that fit.

"Exactly. It's astounding what terrible things can happen when influential people come together for the wrong purposes. The people who wished to harm us have lost power over the years, though we still see the effects of their actions."

"That's awful!"

"It is," Clara agreed. "Many familiars have chosen to work alongside us, as assistance dogs, to help mitigate the damage that's been done. Lola can't bring back my sight, or Coco stop your seizures, nor can they change the way the world has treated us, but they can combine their energy with ours. We're stronger with them here."

Adeline reached for Coco, stroking his head. He leaned into her, giving her all the comfort he could. "What does all this have to do with the smoke?"

Clara made a noise in her throat. "The illnesses in our family haven't just served as a way for non-magical folk to weaken us. They have also acted as a beacon for those who wish to steal it. They have made visible the invisible." Clara touched her glasses again.

"They can't see whether we're witches, but they can see the disabilities," Adeline said.

"Indeed."

Was that what the smoke wanted – to steal her power?

Had it lain dormant in the house until her seizures and Coco's presence had made it sure she was a witch? Maybe it had done this to others in her family – haunting, or perhaps *hunting* them. All because of stupid prejudices and fear.

"We have to stop it." Adeline felt an intention form in her words. There was power in it, just like the power she'd found when she yelled during the earthquake.

Clara clasped Adeline's hand, and she felt their magic stretch between them. "Together we will fight this," she said.

It wasn't quite the same as the swirling mess of energy that had circled her in the smoke, but Adeline could feel they were stronger together. She couldn't do this alone, but with Coco beside her, and Clara, Lola and even Hemi supporting her, she was powerful.

Clara persuaded Adeline to call Hemi, and he came and picked them up from the park. Adeline tried to stay awake, but even on the short journey home, she felt her head nodding in the car, the effects of the seizure making themselves known, despite Clara and Lola's magical intervention.

When she woke, she was inside on the couch, a blanket over her. Coco and Lola were off duty, chasing each other around the house. She smiled as Coco dashed up to her, pressing his cold wet nose to her face and wagging his tail, delighted to see her awake. He bounded away, then back again bringing Lola with him, excited to have both his human and canine friends in the same place.

"Yes, good boy, good girl," she said, patting both of them. Moments like this, it was hard to remember they were not only working dogs but also magical familiars. When he was in play mode, Coco was just her best friend, and she wondered if that was what she needed most, beyond either literal or spiritual guide.

She eased herself up, rolling out the kink in her neck before making her way into the dining room. Hemi and Clara were sitting at the table, sorting through the box of photos. They'd spread the family tree and the quilt out over the table as well.

"How are you feeling?" Clara asked.

Hemi slid his arm around her waist. She leaned against him, the word "exhausted" coming to mind, but instead she just nodded.

"I'm okay." She rubbed the sleep out of her eyes and attempted to smooth her rumpled work clothes. She didn't hold out much hope of that making her look any tidier. She could feel the warmth on one side of her face, where she'd slept smooshed into the couch cushion, and she suspected her face was probably crisscrossed with red lines from the fabric.

Hemi brushed the hair back from her face and smiled, and suddenly she felt beautiful, despite the post-seizure, crumpled, overheated aesthetic. She dropped her gaze, blushing, and he chuckled, clearly enjoying her shyness.

"Did you find anything?" she asked, sitting down at the table.

Hemi shook his head. "Nothing much. Clara says there's some... energy... coming off that tear in the family tree, but we don't know what it means." He stumbled over the word "energy" as if he had to think carefully about whether it was the right one. She didn't blame him. It was all new to her too.

"And Hemi managed to match up several more of the names on the tree to photos," Clara added.

Adeline smiled at the way they were giving each other credit for their discoveries. She guessed they'd had a rather awkward hour getting to know each other as she'd slept. Not an uncommon occurrence in her life, as her medical episodes often threw together random collections of people, who just happened to be around at the time.

"Oh, and we figured out that the quilt is the family tree too, see? Or at least the first part of it." Hemi traced a finger along one of the lines on the page. "The branches and leaves are the people."

"Wow." Adeline ran her hand over the fabric. She worked her way down the tree, the lines all matching up until she got to her great-great-grandmother. The place where she'd repaired the seam was rough under her hand, her stitches not as even as her ancestor's.

"Hey, I ripped the quilt in the same place the family tree is torn." Adeline shivered a little at the coincidence. If it *was* a coincidence. She wasn't sure those existed anymore. "But I must not have mended it right. The leaves don't match up." The paper tree showed five children born from her great-great-grandparents, but the quilt only showed one.

Hemi frowned. "Maybe the other children were born after she finished making it. See this plain band at the bottom? She must have been planning to add the next generation."

"True." Adeline glanced back at the family tree, peering at the tiny writing. It ended with her mother's generation, her mother never having gotten around to updating it. There was something unsettling about that – neither the quilt nor the family tree finished before the women responsible for updating them passed away.

She touched the page, feeling strangely emotional at seeing the names of her extended family. "What are your parents' names?" she asked Clara. "If you think we might be related, we should see if they're on here. Or your grandparents maybe."

There was a pause, and Adeline sensed from the silence that she'd said something wrong. Hemi went still beside her and she could tell he felt it too.

Clara cleared her throat. "My parents' names were Andrew and Ellen Bates, maiden name Littleton."

Adeline let out a breath. "Were... I'm sorry. I didn't know they'd passed away." Of course she didn't. She hadn't asked anything about Clara's life. The older woman had been so kind, helping her figure out her magic, but Adeline hadn't paid much attention to anything beyond that.

Clara shook her head, in a brushing-it-off gesture Adeline had performed herself far too often. "It was a long time ago."

Adeline reached across the table, taking Clara's hand. She'd said that phrase many times herself too. She suspected she'd even said it to Clara.

It made sense now, why Clara had been so quick to adopt Adeline. She may have had a family that discussed magic openly, rather than being left in the dark about it as Adeline had been, but she was still largely on her own. Perhaps she had been searching for something just as much as Adeline had been.

Lola padded over, leaning her head in Clara's lap, as if sensing her mistress's sadness. Clara stroked her head. "Besides, Lola's my family now."

Adeline smiled. She felt the same way about Coco. "The family you choose is the more important one, I think."

Clara made a soft noise of agreement, then cleared her throat. "You should look at the photos Hemi found, see if any of them are the ghost you saw." Clara's tone had an air of clearing away the earlier conversation, and Adeline took it as a signal to move away from the more emotional subject.

Adeline leaned over the table, scanning the photos, paying particular attention to the women, especially the ones Hemi had placed next to her great-great-grandmothers' names. She studied each of them carefully, but then shook her head. "No, none of them are the ghost."

Hemi handed her a sepia-toned image. "I found a clearer one of Millicent. Are you sure it's not her?" Hemi rubbed her back, as if worried the question would offend her.

The photo was a formal, posed photo of Millicent leaning against what looked like the edge of a chest of drawers. She wore a dark dress, with a white broach at the neck, and a tall, ornate hat. Best dress for the occasion of having a photo taken, Adeline guessed. The clothes were similar to the style of the ones the ghost wore, but the face was still wrong. The woman in the photo had strong, striking features – thick dark eyebrows and piercing eyes. The ghost's face was softer, somehow, her eyes and lips more hesitant – unsure of herself.

"Yeah, I'm sure."

Clara and Hemi each let out a breath, the afternoon of fruitless searching weighing on them.

Hemi gestured to a pile of photos at the edge of the table. "There were some I couldn't match up. And I couldn't find the photos we were looking at last night."

"Oh, they're here." Adeline took the photos from her pocket. "I brought them to the park in case you could read something from them," she said to Clara. "But I forgot with everything that happened."

She placed the photos of Millicent and Charles back on the family tree, next to their names. She was struck again by how severe looking her great-great-grandfather was, but she supposed old photos often looked that way, when the subjects had to hold still for so long. Even so, there was something imposing about him. She found herself glad the ghost wasn't the one married to him. He seemed too harsh a person for the hesitant spirit she'd seen.

"Could the ghost have been the generation before?" Clara asked.

Adeline shrugged. "Maybe." There weren't many photos that far back, so she had little to go on. "But the ghost's clothes were like Millicent's, same era, I think." Who was the mysterious woman? She'd felt so certain that the ghost was her great-great-grandmother. It unsettled her to know she was wrong, even though the belief had no basis in the first place.

Her eye fell on a pile of photos to the side. "You said these are the ones you couldn't match up?"

Hemi nodded. "Yeah. Some of them don't have names on them, or the names don't line up with…" Hemi trailed off, noticing Adeline had gone quiet.

"What is it?" Clara asked, her voice sharp. Coco and Lola padded back into the room, both coming to sit quietly beside Adeline. Coco nudged her hand with his nose, rein-forcing what Adeline already knew.

"This one," she said, holding up the photo. "This is my great-great-grandmother."

The photo was faded, showing only a woman's face in profile. The soft features of the ghost stared off to the side, as if looking at something beyond the edge of the frame.

Hemi took the photo from her, frowning. "Not according to the names on the tree. It says Jenny on the back." Hemi paused, looking at the photo. "Actually it says Jenny – question mark."

"I know, but I'm telling you, that's my great-great-grand-mother." Adeline was absolutely sure now, but Hemi didn't seem to be getting it.

What did the question mark mean? Had the person who labelled it been uncertain, even as they wrote it? As a child, her grandma had told her family stories, showing her the photos and sewing box as she did, but it was too long ago. She heard her grandma's voice in her mind, but the words were muffled, dampened by too many years for her to fully recall.

"Can I hold it?" Clara took the photo, clasping it between her palms. She went very still, and Adeline could feel her magic working in the room. It was so strong she was sure even Hemi must be able to feel it.

"I think there's another photo of her." Hemi sorted through the pile. "There was no Jenny on the family tree so I put them..." He cut himself off as he found the second image. In this one, Jenny held a baby. She looked happier, relaxed as she cuddled the small child.

"Yes, that's her. She looks a bit like me, don't you think?" Adeline held the photo up next to her face.

Hemi shrugged. "I guess?"

She could see he wasn't convinced. "Actually, I think she looks like my mum." Though Jenny's face was softer, there was a family resemblance. She'd seen it the first time the ghost appeared. They had the same strong, thin noses and both had a slight quirk to the right bridge above their top lip.

Hemi placed the photos of Millicent and Jenny next to each other. "Could they be sisters, maybe?"

"Maybe?" Adeline wasn't sure. When placed side by side, there were a few similarities between the two women, but not enough for Adeline to be sure they were related. There definitely wasn't the same resemblance she saw between Jenny and her mother. "Can I see the other photo again?" she asked Clara, but the other woman didn't answer. "Clara?"

The photo between Clara's hands was glowing with the power she was pulling from it. She stood, transfixed.

"Clara!" Hemi moved to pull the photo from her, but Adeline stopped him.

"Don't!" She glanced at Lola, and saw the dog was staring intently at her mistress, alert but unconcerned. She lowered her voice. "Don't touch her. She knows what she's doing."

Suddenly, the photo flew from Clara's hands, landing on the family tree next to Millicent's. The tape holding the torn page together peeled back, separating the two pieces.

"What the...?" Hemi's eyes bulged as the torn piece of paper shunted across the tabletop. The photos of Charles and Millicent flipped over, landing on the floor.

Jenny's ghost appeared beside the table, and on the other side, Millicent's figure materialised. They reached for each other, but both were whipped away before their hands met.

Clara's aura lit up, the light around her flaring out until

it was almost too intense to look at. She took a shuddering breath and sat down with a thunk. Lola rushed to her side, climbing up and licking her face. Coco and Adeline weren't far behind.

"Water," she gasped.

Hemi disappeared into the kitchen to get it. Clara reached for Adeline's hand, and Adeline grasped hers, allowing the older woman's magic to flow through her. She felt her own aura expand, and images flashed through her mind too quickly for her to process. She stumbled, feeling for a moment like she was going to pass out or have another seizure.

"Danger," Clara whispered. "Danger is coming."

Adeline shivered and let go of Clara's hand, the dizzy feeling easing as she broke the connection. She looked up and saw Hemi standing in the doorway with the glass of water in his hand. He glanced between her and Clara and she couldn't quite read his expression.

"Here." She beckoned him forward, taking the glass from him and placing it in Clara's hands.

Clara drank deeply, some of the energy around her dissipating as she did. "There's a message they're trying to pass on to us, but they can't. There's another force trying to stop them. It's so intense, so, so intense."

Adeline nodded. She'd felt it too. There was a heaviness in the air between them and the ghosts, which wasn't there with Stanley, nor with any of the other spirits she'd encountered.

Hemi cleared his throat. "Perhaps we should leave this for tonight." He looked at Clara. "I can give you a lift home."

Adeline glanced at him. His voice was tight, and his hands were clenched at his sides. She touched his arm and he looked at her, his face softening for a moment. Then he looked back at Clara and the tension returned.

"Thank you. That would be great," Clara said. If she noticed Hemi's mood, she didn't give anything away.

Despite saying she would give it a rest for the night, Adeline found herself poring over the family tree. She picked up the part of the page with Millicent's name on it, now separated from the rest of the document. Was she imagining it, or was the paper slightly different? She held the pieces up, comparing them, but couldn't decide.

She picked up the photo of her great-great-grandfather. She was struck again by how stern he looked. The face seemed familiar, though, almost as if…

A knock on the door startled her, and she jumped, guilty she'd been looking at it again after telling Hemi she would stop.

She got up to let him back in, Coco trotting along beside her. She opened the door, and Coco bounced and wiggled as if Hemi had been gone for days not minutes.

Hemi stepped inside, and Adeline noticed again how tense he was. His hands had twisted up into tight knots, and he was jiggling. "What the hell was that, Adey?' He unclenched his fist briefly to pat Coco's head, acknowledging the dog's attempts to show him a soft toy. He picked up the photos from the floor, glancing at them and shaking his head.

"What do you mean?" Adeline reached out, resting her hands on Hemi's arms. He calmed under her touch, letting out a breath.

"All that stuff from Clara, her telling you danger is coming?"

"How much did you see?" she asked him.

He shook his head. "Just the photographs flipping. And that tape peeling back."

Adeline nodded. "The ghosts were here too – Millicent and Jenny this time."

Hemi paced the living room awkwardly. Adeline took his hand, drawing him over to the couch. He sat, but only in that he perched on the edge of the cushion, his tension keeping him upright. "I've been thinking, are you sure about Clara?"

"What do you mean?" Adeline asked again.

Hemi seemed to be struggling for the right words. "I mean… wasn't that weird that she just suddenly mentioned her parents have died? It seems like a big coincidence, don't you think?"

"No… lots of people have dead parents."

"But like, why bring it up now? It's like she's trying to force a connection with you."

"She didn't bring it up, I asked!" Adeline shook her head. "Why would you think that?"

"What if *she's* the one causing this, Adey? You said the ghosts never spoke to you before you met her."

Adeline was struck silent for a moment. "That's not true," she said finally. "I spoke to Stanley before I met her."

"But only just. Doesn't it seem strange to you that she appeared right after this all started happening?"

"Lola told her to come find me."

He frowned. "The dog?"

Adeline glanced at Coco, hoping he wasn't offended by Hemi's tone. She must have left that part out when she'd told Hemi the story earlier. "They're familiars – Lola and Coco. I know it sounds strange but..." She wasn't sure she could explain the bond she and Coco had, nor the way he communicated with her. "I think Clara's right – that she and I are related somehow," she said instead. "I can trust her."

Hemi turned to her, taking her hands in his. "Adey, I know you want that to be true, but I was looking at the names on the family tree while you were talking. Her parents' names aren't on there."

"That doesn't mean anything – Mum never updated it properly." But a seed of doubt was worming its way into her mind. She stood, going back over to the table and staring at the family tree. Her gaze darted over the names, but she couldn't concentrate to read them properly. "Or maybe she's on my dad's side," she added lamely.

Coco let out a whine, and Adeline stroked his head

absently. She picked up a stack of the photos, flicking through them, unsure what she was looking for.

Clara had a much better handle on her powers than Adeline did. Was it possible she could cause the ghosts to appear, or the smoke to swirl around people? Was it possible she'd caused the earthquake?

"Oh god," Adeline whispered. What did she really know about Clara? She'd been so desperate for connection – for family. Had she just let a stranger into her life?

"Adey, I'm scared for you."

Adeline stared at Hemi. If she couldn't trust Clara, could she really trust Hemi either? He'd been there at the super-market when this all started after all. She stepped away from him. Perhaps he was trying to drive a wedge between her and Clara to stop her from discovering the truth.

The photos slipped from her hands, scattering across the floor. She dropped to her knees, trying to gather them up as if she could fix everything by fixing this.

"Adey..." Hemi reached down to help her, but she pushed his hand away.

"Don't, I've got it."

"For god's sake, Adeline, why does it always have to be such a battle? Why won't you let me help you with anything?"

Coco leapt up, gripping Adeline's sleeve in his teeth. Adeline looked down. Hemi still held the photo which had flown from the table, and smoke curled its way up his arm from it. She gasped and snatched it from him, tossing it to the floor. Coco let go, satisfied that she was listening. The photo landed face down, and the energy in the room seemed to change as soon as it did.

She looked back at Hemi. He shook himself, his anger dissipating. "It's here isn't it?" he asked.

Adeline nodded. "In the park – I had the photos when the smoke was swirling around me." She'd known she recognised the face that had formed in the smoke around the cocker spaniel's owner.

"Is it Jenny?"

Adeline shook her head. She already knew without seeing it, but she turned the photo over with her toe anyway. Her great-great-grandfather, Charles – Mr Moustache Man – stared up at her, his severe gaze judging them.

"It's him," she said. "He's the ghost."

CHAPTER NINE

*H*emi had a shift. He wanted to call in sick and stay with Adeline, but she sent him off. They hadn't really resolved the argument, merely accepting that they were both stressed and perhaps being influenced by Charles's spirit in the photo, but there was more that needed to be said before they would be able to fully let it go.

Hemi promised that he would text at the end of his shift and come back over if she was still up. She had no idea whether she would be. Her brain was a strange mix of bone-tired exhaustion and wired jitters. She couldn't tell which was winning, but she had a feeling when the exhaustion finally did take over, it would be absolute, and she'd wake up hours later having no memory of falling asleep.

A part of her hoped she would be in bed by the time he finished work. She was still kind of mad at him for not trusting her judgement and accusing Clara. She also felt edgy about his comment that things were a battle with her. Suddenly, their running joke about him rescuing her took on a different meaning.

This was certainly the strangest set of first dates she'd ever had with someone. *Had* they even had a date? It felt like they'd gone from not speaking for years to half relationship, half supernatural detective partnership in a matter of days.

Adeline made herself some food and gave Coco his dinner, then wandered the house, unable to settle anywhere. She looked at the photos again, but they gave no new clues. Coco kept pacing back and forth, not settling either. She wasn't surprised. He was more sensitive to the magical elements than she was, so he must be feeling all of it twice as strongly.

After doing yet another lap around the house, Adeline noticed Coco was no longer following her. Instead, he was sitting by the sewing box, staring at her intently. With everything that had happened, Adeline had nearly forgotten about it. But Coco had been telling her all along that it was important. She stared at it for a while, then gingerly picked it up. When nothing happened – no shaking nor ghost appearing – she took it over to the couch and sat down with it on her lap.

Coco bounded over, excited now she was listening to him. He jumped up on the couch, settling beside her as she psyched herself up to open the box. He propped his head up on her knee, watching with interest as she took the lid off and sorted through the items inside.

There was no rumbling this time, and the box didn't go flying from her hands. Adeline paused a moment, just in case, but everything stayed calm.

There was nothing of interest in the sewing box, or at least not in the supernatural sense. The box's contents were almost a replica of Adeline's own sewing kit. The items were older of course, and in many cases more ornate. Adeline spent a long time staring at a pair of embroidery scissors, which were shaped like a tiny bird. The eye was a blue and red stone, set into the hinge, and Adeline found herself mesmerised by it. She opened and closed the blades, making the bird's beak creak open as if begging for food. She was fascinated by the intricate details of the tool, and she spent far too long playing with them.

Coco nudged her hand, and she finally put them down, knowing that, as beautiful as the scissors were, they were not what she was looking for. Her tired brain was latching on to anything shiny. She picked up the spools of thread next. The ends had come loose, tangling together like a Gordian knot. She picked at them, then lifted the whole mess from the box, beginning the slow, meticulous process of untangling them.

Coco made a little whimpering noise.

"Shh, puppy," she said, stroking his head.

He whined again, louder this time.

"Shh, you've had your dinner already."

She focused on the knot, managing to pull a blue thread free. The whine in Coco's throat rose, but she ignored him.

She followed a red thread as it wove in and out of the other colours, twisting back around on itself.

Coco's paw appeared on hers. She pushed it off, her attention focused on winding the red spool. Coco sat up, barking at her. She looked up, startled. He nipped at her, not making contact, but feigning as if he would bite.

She dropped the box, suddenly noticing how dark it had become. "How long have I been sitting here?" she asked Coco.

He wagged his tail, pleased she was finally paying attention to him and not the cotton. She glanced back at the box, and the bird's eye caught her gaze again.

"It's magic, isn't it?" she said aloud. Coco wagged his tail again, in response.

She picked the box up carefully, avoiding looking at either the knot of thread or the scissors. They weren't what she was searching for, that much was obvious, but they were doing their utmost to keep her distracted. Whoever this box had belonged to, it had a very clever magic indeed.

Adeline closed her eyes, pulling something out of the box at random. Her hands closed on some pieces of fabric. She opened her eyes but glanced at Coco before looking down at the material. He seemed to approve, settling down with his head on her knee again. The pieces were small, just scraps really, but Adeline could see they were left over from the quilt. Was this what he wanted? Was she supposed to fix the quilt with this? Coco's head was heavy on her knee, which seemed to indicate he wanted her to stay where she was.

Adeline peeked carefully back into the box and saw another much smaller patchwork folded up inside. Coco made an approving rumble in his throat.

"This is what you wanted me to find?" she asked him.

He shifted, as if nodding his head. She couldn't deny that she agreed. There was a weight to the work – not literally, it was just a small, unfinished quilt, but she could feel the energy of it. The magic in the scissors and the tangle of threads had kept it disguised before, but now it was in her hands, she knew it had been calling to her all along.

"What does it mean?" she asked Coco. But he had relaxed now he'd gotten his message across, and his eyes were drooping as he slipped towards sleep.

She ran her hand over the patchwork. It was a simple design – eight blocks of nine squares sewn together, each block separated by a band of thinner, oblong tiles in a paler fabric. The ninth block was left unfinished, leaving a jagged edge where the fourth corner should be. It made her feel odd to see it like that – left forever unfinished, as if the time spent labouring over the tiny stitches had amounted to nothing. An overwhelming sadness came over her, making her question whether anything mattered. Was her whole life like these stitches? Tiny, painstaking steps which never complete a journey, all of that work amounting to nothing?

She shook herself, trying to brush off the feeling. Clara

said danger was coming, and she couldn't get caught up in self-pity, but the heaviness refused to lift from her mind.

"No," she said to herself. "It's not for nothing."

She reached for the spool of blue thread, which she'd separated from the knot earlier, then picked up the scraps of fabric.

Five squares were missing from the final section of the patchwork. She searched in the sewing box, finding some paper cut to the right size to be used as templates for the fabric. She pinned a piece, then cut around it, sewing through the paper with the blue thread to tack down the edges. Memories of her mother teaching her how to sew came back as she did. She felt their history stretching out around her – her mother teaching her how to sew, her grandmother teaching her mother, all the way back to Millicent... or Jenny maybe. That part was still confusing.

When she'd finished making the square, she sewed it into the patchwork, carefully trying to match her tiny stitches to the original ones. Then she repeated the process, sewing each new square into the quilt as she finished it.

Adeline had always been crafty – always had sewing and knitting projects on the go, just like her mother. But like many other things, she'd stopped when her parents died, barely even picking up a needle to mend her clothes. Now, she could feel her magic growing stronger with each stitch. No... not her magic: that had always been strong, even if she hadn't known it. It was her connection that was growing.

Each stitch tied her to her family, her ancestors, to the earth, and to her past.

The finished patchwork was small, not meant for an adult, but for a baby most likely. She thought of the photo of Jenny, holding her daughter, and she wondered if this had been meant for that little one – the scraps from the larger quilt becoming a tiny matching blanket for her child.

Adeline felt hopeful, the sadness she'd felt at seeing the project incomplete lifting, but there was still something missing. Coco eyed her, but he gave no more clues as to where she should look. Did she need to add more to the quilt? There'd been barely enough fabric to finish the five squares. She picked up another paper square and a scrap of fabric, twisting both in her hands to see if she could somehow stretch the fabric to make it fit.

Coco lifted his head, sniffing the square as if he thought she was holding a treat.

"It's not food, puppy," she told him.

He sniffed it anyway, then looked at her. She glanced down at the piece of paper. It was brown and splotched with age, but she could make out the edge of scrawling handwriting. *Jennifer Littleto.* Littleton – Clara had said that was her mother's maiden name. Was that the connection between them? That Clara was related to Jenny, not Adeline? That didn't seem right. She was sure all three of them were family somehow.

The N was cut off, just like the last letter had been on the end of Millicent's surname. It almost looked like…

Adeline got up, retrieving the family tree from the table. She lined the square up against the family tree. Yes. This piece of paper had once been a part of it!

She turned the baby quilt over, examining the paper templates she had just sewn, and the ones backing the original pieces of the patchwork. The same aged paper peeked out from beneath the folded edges of the fabric.

Adeline carefully cut the tacking stitches, removing the pieces of paper. Coco watched with interest as she laid them out on the table, fitting them back together to recreate the original torn section of the family tree.

She swallowed. *An intention and an action*, Clara had said. And just like that, she understood what she needed to do.

She took another length of thread, stitching the pieces of paper together. Once again, she felt the magic flowing through her, connecting her all the way back. She could feel each of the women who had come before her as if she was sewing their spirits together.

When she'd finished, she sat back, confused by what she saw. For the most part, the family tree remained the same. Except that Jennifer's name replaced Millicent's as having married her great-great-grandfather, and there was only one child underneath their names.

"He tore it after I died." The voice came from the air itself. The sound was crackly, like a cross between a whisper and radio static.

Adeline gasped, scrambling back as the ghost appeared in front of her.

"Jenny?"

The ghost smiled, apparently not offended by Adeline's fear. "You don't need to be afraid. I'm your family."

"I was right – you are my great-great-grandmother?" Adeline asked Jenny. She was embarrassed to find her voice still betrayed how scared she was. She cleared her throat, trying to force a steadiness she didn't feel.

"You're descended from my daughter." Jenny touched the patched pieces of paper, her transparent finger tracing over the names.

"The baby in the photo?"

Jenny nodded, sadness filling her eyes. Millicent appeared beside her, her image materialising much slower this time, giving Adeline time to adjust.

"You *are* sisters!"

The two women smiled at each other, then shook their heads. "Almost," Millicent said. "We grew up together, but we're cousins, not sisters."

That explained the different last names. Millicent's face was lined now, having lived longer than her cousin, but when they smiled, Adeline saw the resemblance she'd been trying to find earlier.

"And Clara is descended from your side of the family," she said to Jenny.

The ghost nodded. "Yes, you two are cousins as well."

Relief washed through Adeline. The connection she'd felt was real – her family was real.

"After I died, it was decided Millicent would come to

help look after my child." Jenny's outline wavered, blurring a little. It clearly pained her to talk about her daughter. "Eventually she was persuaded to marry Charles."

"But why was that covered up? Why change the family tree?"

They looked at each other again. "He wanted my power," Jenny said eventually. "I had always been sick – seizures like yours – and he'd heard the rumours about the magic in our family, that the disabilities and powers run together. His own magic was weak, and he grew jealous and angry when he discovered he was right about mine. He tried to take it from me, tried to make me use it to his advantage. But when he made me use my power like that… it made me sicker."

Was this what it would have been like for Adeline, if she'd grown up with epilepsy in an earlier time? She didn't even want to think about it.

"He changed the family tree to cover up killing you," she whispered.

Jenny nodded. "I think so, yes. He knew family was important to our magic, and that cutting me off from them would help him control it. But it also killed me."

An intention and an action. The tear across Jenny's name had been deliberate.

"He was a cruel man." Millicent reached out, gripping her cousin's hand. "Charles wouldn't even let me tell Jenny's daughter about her mother – she believed she was mine. She never knew. I told our children nothing of our magic."

Adeline remembered what Clara had said about

misusing magic. Was this what had caused her branch of the family to become distanced from it? "But you died! Changing a piece of paper couldn't hide that!"

"His intention was to make people forget. Jenny had always been sick," Millicent said, repeating her cousin's earlier words. "So, no one questioned her death except me. And then they stopped thinking about her at all."

Adeline swallowed. There had been that question mark after Jenny's name on the back of the photograph. Someone had tried to remember.

"He thought he could hide it from Jenny's daughter and use her power instead."

"His own child?!"

Jenny squeezed Millicent's hand. "Millie married him to protect her." A look passed between them, and Adeline could see the weight of all that the two women had sacrificed to protect each other.

Millicent smiled sadly. "Our family were very angry. They hadn't wanted Jenny to marry him, so they were devastated when I said I was going to take her place. They said if I chose to do that, I was on my own."

That must be the family feud Adeline's mother had told her about.

"I lied and told him I had no magic of my own," Millicent continued. "I had none of the illnesses that run in our family, and so he believed me."

Adeline looked back at the bird-shaped scissors. "You hid your magic in the sewing box."

Millicent nodded. "I did. He would have misused it too, otherwise. I bound it into the patchwork, so it would only be found by the right person," she said.

Adeline glanced down at the patchwork in her hands. She'd had the intention of connecting with her ancestors as she finished it. Completing it had released the magic not just to her, but back to Jenny and Millicent as well, allowing their spirits to talk to her in this way.

"And I hid the pieces of the family tree inside it. I wanted Jenny's descendants to know it had been changed. I wanted them to know who she was."

Adeline ran her hand over the place where she'd tried to mend the tear in the quilt. "You trapped Charles's ghost in the patchwork." Adeline thought of the dust which had attached to her when she'd ripped it. If only she'd known at the time what she'd released.

Jenny shook her head. "Not on purpose. I think I was just so focused on wanting to keep my daughter safe, as I stitched, that I put the intention to trap him into the thread without ever meaning to."

Millicent nodded. "I was the same. All I could think as I finished it was that I wanted all of us to be safe from him. Instead, we just bound all of us into the stitches."

Adeline glanced down at the smaller patchwork she'd completed. If only she'd found this one first. "I'm sorry I released him before you."

The women both reached forward, as if to hug Adeline.

She felt the chill of their transparent hands around her. "We're just glad you figured it out."

"What does he want? He's been hitching his way around the city attaching to people. It seems like he wants to take them over."

Jenny and Millicent looked at each other, their fear obvious. "It's what he's always done – taken energy from people."

Was it as simple as that? Adeline had wondered if the ghosts were just following the same routines they'd had in life, forgetting for a while that they were dead. Was Charles merely continuing with his bid for power, following the same destructive pattern he had in life?

"He's been taking magic from us," Jenny said. "Fortunately, most of Millie's was still in the stitching, but it was enough to let him send energy through. He waited for years, watching this side. When you found your familiar, your power grew enough for him to use it. You must have felt it. It makes you feel so cold and alone when someone steals your power."

Adeline shivered. She had felt it, the years of loneliness in the house.

"We couldn't reach you. He was too strong and kept us back. We tried with your mother, too, but her magic was never as strong as yours."

Adeline didn't feel strong. She stroked Coco's head, and he smooched against her. It calmed her slightly, but that was all. He had reconnected her with the magic, but she hadn't known it was happening.

"How do I stop him?" she asked the cousins.

Millicent and Jenny glanced at each other. They hadn't been able to stop him in life, how could they help her now?

"Family," Jenny said finally. "He doesn't understand the meaning of it. Our bond has been what's held him back."

Adeline's heart sank. That was the one thing she didn't have.

"We'll help you in any way we can," Millicent added. Her shape was starting to blur. Adeline rubbed her eyes, then she realised it wasn't her vision.

"Wait, I still have more questions!"

Millicent's figure was already disappearing. Jenny reached out, but her hand passed straight through Adeline.

"I'm sorry. We're tired, and it takes a lot of energy to stay, especially when there are other people around." She glanced towards the door, and a second later there was a knock.

Adeline started at the sound. When she looked back, both ghosts were gone. Coco leapt up, racing out to the hallway. Adeline was slower, shaking out her stiff legs before standing. She limped her way to the door.

"Hey," Hemi said when she opened it, his tone apologetic. "I know I said I'd message, but my phone was dead."

Adeline pulled him into a hug, and he wrapped his arms around her. She sighed, all her earlier anger forgotten. Coco squished his way between their legs, wanting to be included.

"I'm sorry about before," he said. "I trust you, always. If you trust Clara, I trust her too, okay?"

Adeline nodded. She found she was crying.

Hemi stroked her hair. "Are you all right, Adey?"

Adeline nodded, though she wasn't at all sure that was the truth. "I will be," she said.

CHAPTER TEN

*A*deline and Hemi talked late into the night. She told him about the sewing box and her conversation with the ghosts. Like always, he listened without judgement, though she could see some of it was hard for him to wrap his head around. She could also tell he was still wary of Clara's role in all this, but he was willing to trust Adeline, and that was the important part.

He was quiet when she finished explaining. She could see it running through his mind, almost as if he was physically weighing options, discarding each as he found their flaws. She'd been doing the same thing all evening.

He frowned and looked back at her. "Why is he still in Thorndon?"

"Huh?"

"You said you thought he was passing from person to person to gain energy... Why stay in the same area? People must go through here to all parts of the city – he could have followed me around town if he'd wanted to. There must be a reason he's sticking close by?"

Adeline shook her head. "I don't know... I mean, he could be going away and coming back again?" Even as she said it, she knew it wasn't true. She'd seen the smoke too frequently for it to be a coincidence. "Or maybe he can't go too far from the house?" She thought of the smoke that had made its way back under her front door. Perhaps he was still attached to that part of himself. The idea made her shiver.

"Maybe. Or maybe there's something he wants here."

That made Adeline feel sick. He'd already stolen power from hundreds of people, including the two of them, and Jenny and Millicent. What else could he possibly want?

"What about the ghost from the supermarket?" Hemi asked, suddenly.

"What about him?"

"He's obviously been here a long time, and he was the first one the ghost stole from. Maybe he knows something else?"

Adeline went from feeling a little sick to full-on nauseated at the thought of talking to Stanley again. The sensation of the smoke creeping up to cover her face hadn't left her, and she couldn't help reliving the terror she'd felt when his cold, ghostly hands had grabbed her. She nodded anyway, not wanting to crush Hemi's hopes. "Maybe," she said. "I could go to the supermarket tomorrow, try talking to him."

Hemi hesitated, then ran his fingertips down her arm. "I could come with you, if you want?" Hemi's tone was light, but she heard an echo of their earlier argument in his words.

Adeline swallowed the automatic urge to tell him no. She wanted to keep him away from this – to protect him. But at the same time, she needed that protection herself. "Yeah, if you don't mind, that would be good actually. Honestly, I'm kind of scared."

"Of course." Hemi took her hand, squeezing it.

Adeline bit her lip. "Do you really feel everything is a battle with me?" she asked. She blinked quickly, feeling a lump form in her throat.

Hemi closed his eyes, a groan escaping his lips. "No, not at all. That smoke, it… I don't know. I never would have said that otherwise." He lifted her hand to his mouth, kissing the tips of her fingers. "It's just… sometimes I wish you would let me help you with stuff."

"Like what?"

"Like… climbing up on chairs with a busted knee, when I could reach the fuse box for you, or getting up in the middle of the night to go face a ghost in a quilt in the attic."

"The ghost wasn't in the quilt."

He chuckled. "I know, but I mean if I hadn't woken up, would you have even told me what you were doing, or would you have been climbing that ladder in the dark by yourself?" He raised his hands in a frustrated gesture. "I feel like I'm going to turn around one day, and you'll be really badly hurt, and I'll feel like it's my fault for not stopping you."

Adeline frowned. "You make it sound like I'm incompetent."

Hemi sighed. He took her hands again. "I don't think you're incompetent, you're the most capable person I know. You just... You don't have to do everything by yourself, you know? Especially when it comes to fighting ghosts. I can help."

A heavy knot formed in Adeline's stomach and she found she couldn't look at him. "I guess I just worry that it will be too much."

"What will?"

Adeline had surprised herself with the words, but now she'd voiced them, she knew that worry had been nagging at the back of her mind for a while. "My seizures, the ghosts." Adeline raised her hands in an "all of it" gesture. "You're going to have to help me. Hell, you *are* going to have to rescue me sometimes. And I guess I feel like if you help me with the small stuff too, then..." Adeline swallowed, the lump in her throat growing along with the knot.

"Adey..." Hemi scooched closer to her, dipping his head to try and catch her eye. "You could never be too much. I promise."

Adeline felt herself soften. He took her chin in his hand, making her look at him. "I'll make you a deal. I will stop trying to rescue you, if you throw me a bone and let me make your life easier sometimes."

Her mouth twisted into a half smile. "I let you cut the onions for the vegetable bake."

He laughed. "That you did."

"And get my slippers."

"True." His arms slid around her, pulling her into his lap.

She pressed her lips to his in a soft kiss. "And I'll let you fight a ghost with me tomorrow."

They got up early the next morning, both of them yawning and rubbing their eyes, so that they could head to the supermarket before they had to get to work. Adeline felt a little guilty. Her job had not been getting the best of her attention, lately, but she had a feeling that wouldn't be a problem for much longer. Either they would figure this out and defeat Charles's spirit, or... Well, she would cross the "or" bridge if they came to it.

Adeline tried to slip Coco's harness over his head, after putting her own jacket on, but he ducked away from her, going to stand on the other side of the room.

"What's the matter, buddy?" Hemi asked him. "Don't you want to go to work?"

Coco stared at her intently, and Adeline hesitated. "I think he might be trying to tell me something."

Hemi glanced up at her. "Seizure or something supernatural?" He moved to her side, ready to switch gears from friend to paramedic if she went down.

"Supernatural, I think," she said. "I feel fine."

He relaxed a little, though she wasn't sure he should. Were ghosts really any less alarming than unbidden neurological activity?

Coco nudged the sewing box with his nose, then dropped into a down-stay position, staring directly at Adeline. The quilt was on the floor next to the box, and Coco's paw rested on the edge of it.

"I think he wants us to take these with us." Hemi picked up the box. The bird-shaped scissors were sitting on top, and Adeline saw them catch Hemi's eye. He stared at them, becoming transfixed as she had done last night. She grabbed the scissors, wrapping her palm around the blue and red eye.

Hemi blinked, shaking himself slightly, but he didn't seem aware of what had happened.

"That's not a bad idea," she said, pocketing the scissors.

Adeline swore she heard the store manager sigh the moment she and Hemi entered the supermarket. She couldn't help but laugh as she thought how it must look, with her carrying a quilt. Perhaps he thought she was planning to have a nap in his store, this time, not just collapse.

Hemi glanced at her as she giggled, but she didn't

explain. She handed him a shopping basket instead, hoping to dissuade the gawking customers by just going about their business.

"Do you need anything?" she asked Hemi. She figured she could at least make herself useful, while they went on a ghost hunt.

He stared at her, bemused. "We're not here to shop, Adey."

She shrugged. "Two birds, one stone."

Coco trotted around the aisles, happy now he recognised a familiar routine. He was such a good boy, Adeline thought. When this was all over, she'd have to get him a special treat or a new toy. She let out a breath. She tried not to let herself think of the possibility that this might all be over soon – she didn't want to jinx it.

They made their way around the aisles, Adeline picking out items for both of them, as Hemi listed off what he needed – a lot as it turned out. Groceries hadn't exactly been the priority for either of them lately, and besides, she'd interrupted his last attempt at shopping when she collapsed.

Adeline kept an eye out, but so far, there had been no sign of Stanley.

"Where was he, when you saw him last?" Hemi asked.

"The bread aisle." Adeline shivered, remembering his cold hand grasping her. Hemi moved closer, replacing the memory with his own warm touch.

It wasn't as comforting as she'd hoped, but she forced a reassuring smile and led him to the bread aisle anyway, swallowing her fear as she looked around. "He's not..." She cut herself off as a swirl of smoke appeared in front of them. "Stanley," she said, as he materialised in front of them.

Adeline glanced down at Coco. His ears were pricked, and his eyes wide, staring at the transparent figure in front of them, but he didn't growl. That had to be a good sign. Hemi simply shivered, unable to see or hear the ghost but sensing him anyway.

"It's not the same," Stanley said. "None of it's the same." He started his confused pacing, before he noticed Adeline. "Oh..." his eyes went wide, "it's you!"

He didn't seem to see Hemi, nor Coco.

"He's here," Adeline told Hemi. He nodded, then glanced around, noticing the other shoppers still staring at Coco. He moved to stand on the other side of Stanley, positioning himself so that it would look like Adeline was talking to him.

Even with the cover, Adeline struggled to know what to say. She realised she was angry with Stanley. Very angry.

"Why did you do that to me?" she hissed at the ghost. "Why did you help him?"

He drew back, his outline wavering as if he was thinking of disappearing. Coco nudged Adeline's hand, leaning lightly against her leg. She took a breath, running her hand over his head, calming herself.

"Stanley," she said, keeping her voice measured. "My great-great-grandfather is bouncing around like a supernatural hitchhiker, and I need you to tell me what you know."

The ghost nodded. "That's fair, that's fair. But it's not the same. None of it's the same." He went back to his pacing.

Adeline sighed. This seemed to be a loop he got stuck in. She looked to Hemi, knowing he couldn't hear the ghost. "He just keeps saying nothing's the same."

Hemi frowned and glanced around. "I guess he's confused by the supermarket, if he died before it was built."

That made sense. Thank goodness one of them was able to think practically!

"It's a shop," she told Stanley. "It was built here after you died." Was it insensitive to mention a ghost's death? She opened her mouth to apologise, but Stanley stopped his pacing.

"Yes," he said. "Yes, that's right, I remember now." He turned his focus back to Adeline, seeming calmer now. Then he frowned. "But you're not dead."

"No, I'm not."

"Then how do I know you?"

Adeline closed her eyes in a slow blink, trying desperately not to lose her temper. "We met the other day. You grabbed me and helped my great-great-grandfather steal some of my energy." Adeline found she was tapping her hand against her side each time she said "great-great", turning it into a rhythm of sorts. She lowered her voice. Even if people did think she was talking to Hemi, rather than thin air, she still sounded nuts.

"Please, Stanley, can you help us? We want to know what he's doing... why he's hanging around."

"Hmm… nasty ghost, I remember now. Oh, but it's all so different. None of it's the same," Stanley started again.

Adeline sighed. "You died, Stanley. It's different because you're a ghost." She didn't like the harsh tone coming out of her mouth, but she needed him to focus. "What can you tell me about my great-great-grandfather?" She tapped her hand with the words again, and the sound seemed to focus Stanley.

"Oh yes, that's right. He stole my energy. That's why I'm muddled."

Adeline doubted that – he'd seemed thoroughly befuddled when she first met him.

"He came here with someone… his daughter. Or grand-daughter."

Close enough, Adeline thought. "Yes, that's me."

"He wanted her power, but…" Stanley trailed off.

"But…?" Adeline prompted.

"He wasn't strong enough to take it, so he took some of mine first. He said if I didn't help him, he'd take all of it."

That explained why Stanley looked so scared when they'd first met. "But what did Charles want with it? And why is he still hanging around?"

"He wanted her power."

"You've already told me this, Stanley."

Hemi moved to stand beside Adeline as her temper flared up again.

She took a breath. "And it's already happened. He took some of my power, then some of half the city's."

Stanley shook his head. "No not that power. He came back – kept coming back with different people. He wants all of it. Had to be strong to take it."

"He wants all of what?"

"Her power. Had to take all of it for it to work."

Adeline's stomach lurched. "He wants to take all my energy?"

Adeline felt Hemi tense beside her. He gripped her arm, as if he could protect her by his mere presence, but what chance did he stand against a ghost he couldn't even see?

She squeezed his hand, reassuring him as much as seeking it herself. What exactly would it mean for her if Charles took all her power? Even the small amounts he'd stolen so far had left her drained and sick.

"Not you," Stanley said. His voice was hesitant, and he frowned as he tried to put it all together. "Not you, he said there was another."

"Clara?" Adeline wasn't sure if that was better or worse. Clara stood more of a chance of being able to stop Charles, but her magic was so much stronger. What would he be able to do with that amount of power?

But Stanley was shaking his head. "No, no, the first one. The power he's always wanted."

"Jenny," Adeline breathed. That's why Charles's spirit had come back to the house. He hadn't been trying to stop Adeline releasing Jenny and Millicent's spirits, he'd just been trying to delay Adeline from undoing the spell, until he'd gained the strength he needed to take Jenny's power from her.

Stanley was disappearing, the soft wisps of his outline fading into nothing. Adeline thought of trying to hold him there, using her magic to pull the last shreds of information from him. But she could see the ghost was tired and confused. More than that, he was afraid. How many times had Charles come through here, stealing energy from him, and anyone else he could?

Coco stared up at Adeline, waiting for a command or signal for what he should do. Adeline stared back at him, wondering the same thing. She looked to Hemi. If Charles was strong enough now that he could siphon off Jenny's magic, then what could he do to a living person? Adeline had seen how ill Hemi looked after his last contact with the smoke. Could she put him at risk again? He hadn't heard what Stanley had said. She could send him off with a witchy-sounding task – ask him to buy some sage or tell him to go find the magical supplies shop to keep him occupied, while she went back and protected Jenny and Millicent.

Hemi's hand moved on her arm, gently stroking her skin, reassuring her. She met his eyes. He stared back at her, his tension and fear evident. She could see how much he wanted to pull her away – how much he wanted to take her away from all of it. But he didn't. He was keeping his promise – not trying to rescue her. And now she had to keep hers.

She took his hand. "We have to get back to the house," she told him. Coco wagged his tail, agreeing with her.

Hemi nodded and put down the shopping basket. "What did Stanley say?" His hand moved to the small of her back, guiding her towards the exit.

"I'll explain on the way, but I think he's going to go after Jenny." Adeline was concerned for the fate of her ancestor's spirit, of course, but she was also worried about what Charles intended to do with the power. He'd killed Jenny once already, in his quest for stronger magic – what other destruction would he cause once he had it?

Hemi frowned, his expression grim. "Should we call Clara for help?" he asked, but Adeline was already turning to Coco.

"Where's Lola?" she asked Coco. "Can you find Lola?"

Coco's tail wagging went into double time and he set off, glancing back at her and Hemi every few steps to make sure they were following.

Coco led them towards the park. For a moment, Adeline wondered if he was really taking them towards Clara, or if he just wanted to play. Then she saw a flash of red hair and Lola's tail peeking up from the other side of the bank.

"Clara!" she called, not wanting to startle her. "It's me, Adeline, and Hemi. We have to get back to my place." She didn't bother trying to explain, simply reaching out and taking Clara's hand. Her heart was racing, and she desperately wanted to be moving, but she forced herself to stand still – to give Clara a chance to glean the information she needed. Hemi watched this, clearly confused, but trusting that she and Clara knew what they were doing.

Clara took a sharp breath in. "Come on, let's go."

They made their way across the bridge over the motorway, back to Adeline's house.

"The smoke is moving towards us," Clara said. "I can feel it coming."

Adeline could feel it too, like a tingling itch at the back of her mind. She clutched the quilt closer to her chest. They had to get back to the house before it did. They couldn't let the two parts of the ghost join back together, and they really couldn't let Jenny or anyone else get caught in the middle of it.

The tingling got stronger the closer to home they got. Adeline could feel the two parts of the smoke reaching for each other, their terrible mess of energy becoming stronger by the minute. Adeline paused. *Both* parts of it were becoming stronger. That must mean the part in the house had already started feeding on Jenny.

"What do we do?" Hemi asked Clara. "How do we stop this?"

Clara just shook her head. "I don't know. I can feel all the pieces of the solution, but I don't know how they fit together."

Adeline understood. All the energy from the people

Charles had stolen from was vying for Adeline's attention, and her connection to it was only surface level. It must be incredibly intense for Clara feeling all of it.

Lola and Coco stopped on the street outside Adeline's house, refusing to go any closer. Hemi started up the stairs, but Adeline gripped his arm.

"Don't," she whispered. The smoke crept out from under the door, swirling in front of it like a forcefield.

Clara seemed to sense it, drawing back, her posture stiffening. "Can you see the smoke anywhere else, Adeline? I can feel the other part of it is near."

Adeline scanned the area around them. "No, I can't. There's no one…" Adeline trailed off as someone familiar came into view – Dana.

Her co-worker had her headphones in, bopping to her music as she walked towards them in her cheerful Dana way. But there was something wrong. The bubbly orange glow Adeline had seen around her at work was murky, the colour muddied by the swirling grey coils wrapped around her.

"Dana," Adeline whispered. She broke away from Hemi and Clara.

"Adey, wait!" Hemi called, but Adeline kept going.

Dana looked up as Adeline approached her, her face breaking into a smile. "Hey chicky, are you feeling b—"

Adeline threw the quilt at Dana, wrapping it around her.

"What the hell, Adeline?!" Dana struggled against the weight of the blanket, unable to find the edge.

Clara and Lola caught up to them. "What are you doing?"

"I trapped her in the quilt," Adeline said. Clara had said the action to create magic could be anything, as long as the intention was clear, but already Adeline could see it wasn't working. The coils of smoke were seeping out, extending their reach around Dana's covered form.

"That won't work. We need to bind him," Clara told her.

"What is the matter with you?!" Dana finally found the edge, pulling the fabric away from her face. "Why would you do that?" she shrieked, glaring at Adeline.

Adeline just shook her head, knowing there was no way she could explain it. Dana frowned, turning away.

"No, Dana, don't!" Adeline reached out to grab Dana before she got close to the house, but Dana was still angry. She jerked away from Adeline's touch, moving closer to the stairs in the process.

The smoke darted out from her, sliding under the door before Adeline could stop it.

"No!" The realisation that she'd failed hit Adeline like a physical blow. She doubled over, her hands pressing hard against her temples as she tried not to cry.

Dana's face morphed from anger to concern. She stepped towards Adeline, reaching out. "What's happening, are you having a seizure?"

Adeline pulled away from her and stumbled up the stairs to the house.

"What the hell is going on?" Dana yelled.

Adeline didn't have time to answer. Coco and Hemi

followed her up the stairs. Clara stepped towards Dana, clasping her hand when she found it, and gently removing the quilt from her shoulders.

Hemi reached for the doorknob, but Adeline grabbed his hand. "Don't! It's covered in the smoke."

They peered through the glass panel instead. Adeline could see Jenny's figure materialising in the hallway, the smoke circling her.

"Woah," Hemi whispered.

Adeline glanced at him, alarmed. "You can see them?"

"Yeah."

That was not a good sign. Adeline had been worried about what Charles would do with the energy he was stealing. Using it to physically appear in the world was a very bad start. Coco whimpered, cowering down and hiding between Adeline's feet. She'd never seen him so afraid, and the sight scared her more than anything else.

Jenny looked up, staring through the glass at Adeline. Her face distorted, the wispy outlines of her form twisting in pain. Millicent appeared beside her, but the smoke lunged at her, and she was thrown back, dissolving in the air as she flew through it.

"No!" Adeline reached for the door.

"Adey, you can't!"

Hemi grabbed her, holding her back just like she had done herself, a moment before.

"He's hurting her!"

The smoke was becoming thicker, swirling and twisting

as it swarmed around Jenny. Her outline grew fainter as his strengthened.

Adeline felt for her keys in her pocket, her hands closing on the bejewelled bird scissors instead. She stared at them, a plan forming in her mind. "I have to go in there," she told Hemi. She kept her voice steady, leaving no room for him to argue. "Please don't try to stop me."

He stared at her, slowly shaking his head. "You can't," he repeated.

Adeline turned away from him, though it pained her to do it. She reached for the door, but he grabbed her keys before she could.

She scrambled to grab them back. "I have to!"

Hemi stared at her for a moment, then unlocked the door himself, the smoke swarming over his hand as he did.

"Hemi!" She reached for him, but he backed away, keeping the smoke from her. His skin turned grey as he paled.

"Go. Stop him."

He stumbled backwards, dropping the sewing box in the doorway, scattering the items inside. Adeline felt like he was wrenching her heart out of her body. She couldn't leave him like this.

"Go, Adeline," Clara called. "Lola and I will look after him."

Adeline swallowed and nodded, even though she knew Clara couldn't see the gesture. She turned away from Hemi, stepping over the fallen sewing supplies and into the house.

Coco followed close at her heels, still afraid but unwilling to leave her.

She held the bird scissors in front of her, letting the light catch the bejewelled eye. "This is what you want, right, Charles? The power?"

If she could just get him to look at the scissors, she was sure he would be mesmerised, just like she and Hemi had been. Then she could draw him away from Jenny. The smoke reversed its swirls, giving the impression of the spirit turning to look at her. Jenny's figure cowered, her trembling form barely visible now.

"It won't work." Millicent's whispery voice came from the air beside Adeline. She turned, and Millicent's figure began to materialise. "The distraction in the scissors was only ever meant to be temporary. It won't last long enough."

"Then what do I do?" Adeline's voice was choked by the tension in her throat.

"I don't know," Millicent whispered. "I don't know." She was crying, her ghostly tears falling from her face and disappearing into the air as they left her body.

Adeline stared at the writhing mess of smoke and energy in front of her. It was so strong now. "There has to be something else!" She dodged around the smoke, returning to the fallen sewing box. Coco followed her, sniffing at the scattered items. "What am I looking for? What am I looking for, Coco?" she asked him. He kept sniffing everything, seeming not to know. None of it looked magical, but nothing ever did.

Through the door, she could see Clara and Lola tending to Hemi. Coils of the warm orange magic wrapped around them, and the colour was slowly returning to his face. Dana stood to the side. She dropped the quilt, and it lay forgotten on the steps, the seam Adeline had mended visible in the bright light.

Adeline turned back to Millicent. "Jenny trapped him in the quilt before. Why didn't it work when I tried to fix it?"

Millicent shook her head. "I don't know. We didn't even know we were doing it."

"We..." Adeline repeated. "You both worked on the quilt?"

Millicent nodded. "Jenny died before she finished it."

Adeline stared at the ghost, things finally falling into place. The smoke towered over Jenny. In life, Charles had been cruel and selfish, trying to steal Jenny's magic, and as a spirit, he was the same. He could take it, but he would never be given it. He would never understand the power and strength that came from true, loving connection. She reached out in her mind, and she felt Clara and Hemi reach back.

You're not alone.

Adeline heard the echo of Clara's earlier words in her head. Hemi had sacrificed himself to the smoke, to get her inside the house. Clara and Lola had found her in the park – they *kept* finding her, every time Coco reached out. And Coco. He was by her side, day in day out. Even Dana was there each day at work, greeting Adeline with warmth and love. She could feel all of them – her chosen family – stretching out along the lines of energy Clara had shown her.

She couldn't do this alone... but she didn't have to.

"Coco, come!" she called.

He bounded to her side, ignoring the smoke. The others followed, crowding inside the doorway.

Millicent seemed to understand what Adeline was doing, and she clasped Adeline's hand, her ghostly fingers wrapping around Adeline's living ones, lending her strength.

Adeline reached into the sewing box again, grabbing the knot of cottons she'd got caught up in trying to untangle. She pulled at the end of one of them, and amazingly, it came loose.

Clara had told her to bind Charles. She didn't know what that meant in magical terms, but she could damn well make it work in literal ones. She looped the end of the thread under and around Coco's collar, attaching it while keeping hold of the spool. "Go!" she told him.

He took off, circling around the smoke, then running back to Adeline. The smoke spun as he did, seeming to watch him.

Adeline took a breath, reaching into the mess of threads, and again, by some miracle, pulling out another one which came free. "Lola," she called, but the familiar was already by her side, bending her head to allow the thread to be attached to her collar. "Go!" she told Lola, and the dog raced in the other direction to Coco, looping the thread and returning to Adeline.

"Good boy, good girl," she told them. She knelt to untie the threads from their collars, clasping the ends and the spools together in her hands, then pulled the loops of thread back, watching as they cut straight through the middle of the smoke. Charles seemed to feel it, the smoke splitting and curling away from the thread.

"You are my family," she told the dogs. They licked her face in response.

"What now?" Hemi asked.

He was standing, thanks to whatever Lola and Clara had done, but she could see he was still weak. This had to end.

"I need the quilt," she told him.

Hemi grabbed it, bringing it inside to her. Adeline grasped his hand, squeezing it, then took the quilt from him. The impulse she'd felt to bring the scissors with her wasn't about the magic held inside, there was a much more practical use for them. She slashed the stitches she'd made to repair the quilt, letting the tear hang open once more.

"An intention and an action," she said.

Clara nodded, understanding dawning on her. "But it has to be the right action."

"It has to be all of us," Adeline said, looking at each of her friends in turn. She remembered how she hadn't let Hemi help her mend the tear the first time. Her refusal to take help had almost cost them, but not this time.

Adeline grabbed a needle, threading the ends of both

reels of cotton through the eye at the same time and then cutting a length. Hemi held out the quilt to her.

Adeline took a breath, making sure the intention was clear in her mind. "Jenny is my family, Charles. Not yours," she told the smoke.

She stuck the fabric with the needle, bringing the two sides of the tear together with the thread to make the first stitch. Around her, the walls began to rumble as Charles fought back, but Adeline ignored them. Coco and Lola lay down on either side of her, giving her strength. She looped the thread several more times, making a row of wonky stitches, then she passed the needle to Hemi.

He blinked at her, not understanding.

Adeline wavered, feeling all of the magic both good and bad in the room. "Help me, Hemi," she whispered. "I want you to help me."

Finally, he nodded. He took the needle from her, and followed her actions, sticking the fabric and making the next set of stitches. Then he passed the needle to Clara, and gently guided her hand to the tear. She felt along it, carefully mending her part of the seam by touch alone. She passed the needle to Dana.

"Me?" Dana's face was white, and her hands were shaking.

Adeline nodded, encouraging her. "It needs to be all of us."

Dana shook her head, her normally bright aura paling as she tried to make sense of the supernatural chaos around her. But she took the needle anyway, steadying her trembling hands to sew.

"Now you." Adeline turned to Millicent.

The ghost's eyes widened. "But I can't hold it."

Adeline squeezed Millicent's hand, her fingers passing straight through Millicent's ghostly ones. "We can do it together."

Millicent glanced at Jenny's faint form, and the cousins nodded to each other. Adeline took the needle from Dana, and Millicent placed her hand over Adeline's, the transparent outline of her fingers disappearing into the flesh. Together, they made the last stitch, closing the tear.

The finished seam was nowhere near as neat as it had originally been, now even worse than Adeline's patch up job. But it had been made with all of them, one thread connecting the family Adeline had made for herself.

She looked at each of them in turn, letting them help her, joining their energy to hers. "They are *my* family, Charles, not yours."

The smoke became agitated, and the ground began to rumble again. "They are my family," she said, using it like a mantra as she had done during the earthquake. "They are *my* family."

The rumbling increased, knocking Clara and Dana off their feet. The dogs began to howl, and Hemi grabbed Adeline, keeping her upright.

"Drop, cover, hold," Adeline yelled, sure of herself now, her intentions and actions clear. "Drop, cover, hold. Drop, cover, hold." She took a breath. The magic was in her; in her family and everything they shared. "Stop, cover, hold," she whispered.

With a rush, the smoke spooled away from Jenny, coiling around the thread in the quilt. Adeline quickly bundled it up, folding it so that the mended seam wasn't visible.

Hemi stumbled, falling to his knees, and Adeline fell with him.

She could hear the others groaning, all of them spent. Adeline reached for Coco, and he licked her face, seeking comfort as much as giving it.

Jenny and Millicent moved towards each other, their ghostly forms embracing, both of them crying. They turned to Adeline as one.

"Thank you," Jenny mouthed, but the sound from her words didn't reach Adeline.

Millicent kissed her fingers, raising them into a wave. Adeline nodded, but tears formed in her eyes. The cousins held hands, as they slowly disappeared.

"Wow," Hemi said.

Adeline turned back to him, as he spoke. He sat on the floor beside her, holding his head. Lola was licking Clara's face, and Clara spoke softly, praising Lola for her help in the rescue.

Adeline crouched beside Hemi, touching his face, gently. "You okay?"

He looked up at Adeline, and a cheeky grin broke through his exhaustion. "Remind me of this – of how fricken awesome you are – if I ever think you need rescuing again."

Adeline cracked up. She pushed his shoulder gently, then pulled him into a fierce hug. He squeezed her back, then his lips found hers. Adeline kissed him just as fiercely as she'd hugged him.

"Um, excuse me!"

Adeline and Hemi broke apart as Dana spoke.

"Is anyone going to tell me what the hell is going on?"

Adeline, Hemi and Clara all laughed, and once they started, they couldn't stop.

"Come on," Adeline said finally. She took Dana's hand and gestured towards the kitchen. "Let's go have a cup of tea, and we'll tell you a ghost story."

Hemi put his arm around Adeline. "Don't forget the witches."

"And the familiars," Clara added, as she picked up Lola's harness. Coco and Lola wagged their tails.

Dana just nodded, too baffled to say anything else.

Adeline took pity on her. "Mostly, it's just a story about family," she said. "The kind you get to choose."

A NOTE FROM HELEN VIVIENNE FLETCHER

Hello! I hope you enjoyed *Familiars and Foes*. This was such a fun book to write, especially as I got to include an assistance dog just like my own dog, Bindi. Having an assistance dog has made a huge difference to my life and because of that, one New Zealand dollar from the sale of each copy goes to the Assistance Dogs New Zealand Trust. Thank you for supporting this great cause!

If you liked *Familiars and Foes*, please consider reviewing it on Amazon or Goodreads. Every review helps!

Want more witchy fiction? Keep reading for a list of all the Witchy Fiction books written by my friends and I here in New Zealand. If you'd like to find out more about us and our books, check out our website at www.witchyfiction.com or find us on Facebook.

ABOUT THE AUTHOR

Helen Vivienne Fletcher is a children's and young adult author, spoken word poet and award-winning playwright. She has won and been shortlisted for numerous writing competitions including winning the Outstanding New Playwright Award at the Wellington Theatre Awards, making the shortlist for the Storylines Joy Cowley Award, and the finalist list for the Ngaio Marsh Best First Book Award.

Helen has worked in many jobs, doing everything from theatre stage management to phone counselling. She discovered her passion for writing for young people while working as a youth support worker, and now helps children find their own passion for storytelling through her work as a creative writing tutor.

She lives in Wellington with her disability assistance dog, Bindi – a five-year-old, playful Labrador who loves soft toys, cuddles, and can fit three tennis balls in her mouth at once.

Overall, Helen just loves telling stories and is always excited when people want to read or hear them.

Find out more at www.helenvfletcher.com.

MORE WITCHY FICTION BOOKS

Need more witchy goodness in your life? Check out the full list of Witchy Fiction books below!

Succulents and Spells (Windflower One), by Andi C. Buchanan: Laurel Windflower is a witch from a family of magic workers - but her own life is going nowhere until Marigold Nightfield knocks on her door. Marigold is a scientist from a family of witches, and she's in search of monsters. What lies ahead could reveal all Laurel's shortcomings to the woman she's trying to impress... or uncover the true nature of her power.

Hexes & Vexes, by Nova Blake: Small towns are full of gossip, and Mia is pretty sure that no one in her hometown of Okato has ever stopped talking about her. Cast off by her best friend, blamed for a local tragedy – Mia had no choice but to run away.

Now, ten years later, she's being dragged back.

Brand of Magic (Redferne Witches, Book One), by K M Jackways: Hazel Redferne is an empath witch but she's given up on magic. When her neighbour, Joel, needs her marketing expertise, Hazel jumps right in to help. But an attack on her powerful aunt means unlocking her psychic powers is the key to protecting the Redferne witches. Can Hazel let magic - and love - back in?

Witching with Dolphins, by Janna Ruth: Friends before magic (or boys) has always been Harper's prerogative. Her best friend Valerie is everything she is not: beautiful, confident, and the most powerful witch on Banks Peninsula. They might not see eye to eye on everything, yet, when a sinister scientist threatens their coven, Harper is willing to give up everything: the man they both love, her life, or even the little magic she has.

Holloway Witches, by Isa Pearl Ritchie: Ursula escapes to Holloway Road leaving her former life in tatters following a bad break-up. She's looking forward to a quiet respite in a cozy cottage with a lush garden and lots of bookshelves, but instead she can't shake the eerie feeling she's being followed...

Overdues and Occultism, by Jamie Sands: That Basil is a librarian comes as no surprise to his Mt Eden community. That he's a witch? Yeah. That might raise more than a few eyebrows. When Sebastian, a paranormal investigator filming a web series starts snooping around Basil's library, he stirs up more than just Basil's heart.

CPSIA information can be obtained
at www.ICGtesting.com
Printed in the USA
LVHW041925091120
671184LV00004B/802